To Eileen and

Best wishes from the

author.

Michael Hillier

17 August 1978

# Come Dance With Me

MICHAEL HILLIAR

Blackstaff Press Belfast

Published by Blackstaff Press Limited, 16 Donegall Square South, Belfast, BT1 5JF

ISBN 0 85640 100 5

Printed in Northern Ireland by Belfast Litho Printers Limited.

I am of Irlaunde,
Ant of the holy londe
Of Irlande.
Gode sire, pray I thee,
For of saynte Charite,
Come ant daunce wyt me
In Irlaunde.

The chocolate and gold State Highway Patrolman gazed down at him lying beside the tangled red Parisienne Convertible, coming to could see this flabby head shaking 'He's a goner for sure!'

He remembered the sign to Sedalia and faintly thought what a ridiculous place to die on Interstate 70 to Kansas City on such a hot summer's day. The car radio was still on and seemed louder —

'It takes a worried man to sing a worried song,
I'm worried now, but I won't be worried long . . .'

It was only too true — but it didn't really matter as they lifted him into the ambulance to shriek away, swaying white and blinking red — angry angel! Another face, faces floating, a face like St Peter's perhaps, praying, no, adjusting the pain, he travelled back, as always back to that day his mother said was born the mad dog was howling at the soft morning moon. It was September with the first tints of golden on green, faded days, protesting loudly as the sun began to rise from sea pushing night from Strangford to the West. Crows were gathering black on an aqua sky — echoed the broken ivy walls and tumbled moss graves at all angles as if earth had suddenly moved the weathered and long forgotten names in Ireland — was his beginning.

Were phantoms on foggy Belfast streets? Mysterious hunched figures glide along the narrow red bricked rows; grouped at corners the mumbled words rise meaningless. Sulphur eyed, symbol of Satan stares a big white owl in the fir tree plantation. Seems like a bold wicked rooster — struts on the ancient dung heap; crippled runt pig lies sleeping in fallen over disused churn. And that mask, so sinister and cold, a metal skull the yawning sockets hinting hell on earth, men on broken bone horizon about to do battle, blessed by crooked priests, is their awful cry . . . still there no doubt, glass case the Ulster Museum.

Evening comes the milky mist filling each little hollow and valley, then bed by candle-light makes giant dancing shadows up the narrow creaking stairs. Rain on sagging slate roof, hurrying fat clouds, old home quietened, mice beneath the floor. His familiar voice somewhere, and dream, dream laughter in buttercup fields and purple mountains; see sparkling clear streams and bright spotted trout in deep pools lie, is a mysterious Round Tower across Narrow Water. Castle full of memories, too many memories — memories of red red blood on the green green land . . . and woman crying softly somewhere.

Farm's morning sounds fill the flower papered room — smells of sweet pea. Open window and let a butterfly free, flutters down like an autumn leaf, wonder where will it go? In the kitchen fire is well lit warming porridge to spoon with new made blackberry jam, drink weak tea; gaze at Adolf Hitler makes a point — arm raised from last Friday's *News Letter*.

Outside make for the byre — can hear Finn milking two steady pulsing streams. So dark at first in there and no knowing what could be underfoot, the dog, cat, rat, rake . . . remember old Rory lost the tip of his tail from a falling slasher once. Sudden foul eruptions all sides, then there's pigeons above, pigeons that Finn took to Omagh in a bag to try to get rid of once, were home the same day! His strong shoulder bent into warm cow's side, sitting on an upturned bucket whistling some Orange tune — the cows will give more milk! Strange docile creatures that fly in the night! Then to get them from byre to back field before they mess, as one always does.

Finn next mixes meal and potatoes with long iron rod in coffin like bath, fills buckets and disappears underneath the loft to feed madhouse of pigs — would eat him alive they seem so hungry. Think how brave he is to go all alone amongst them, and what a good place it would be to throw Judas or the Pope!

Uncle Finn and Father Christmas are the two finest men in the whole wide world!

Ploughing in March with a one furrow plough, horse strains to shouts — a language only both can understand. Sounds of cutting metal against earth turning brown from stubble grey. Scatter of gulls in from the coast, men ditching fields away, fields where Patrick preached; bonfire smoking slowly low across rolling hedgescape. The golden haired boy swinging on gate — can see from its thick pillars Ballynoe Stone Circle in the distance . . . an unknown presence, unreasonable force, place where things happened, happen? In the wink of an eye past is present; aware already of those have gone before this island.

By Patrick's day is luck to have the fields sown, up and down his measured strides scattering seed from whirring fiddle. God help the man who'd cross that path! Harrow it under and make a scarecrow. Soon haze to lush green, August colours ripe and ready to cut with Hogg's most wonderful binder and Fordson tractor — lies all night in the yard to amaze and pretend on springy cast-iron seat. Starts with a roar of thick smoke morning after dew has lifted; around the first swathe, without a doubt the most exciting sight ever to see, sweet smell of twine, corn and carbon monoxide. After an hour or so men stop for tea and sandwiches, talk terrible wise — remember days when work was done with billhook or scythe; throw wet tea leaves on the ground and say tea trees will grow! Underneath chipped stone find fragments of deep blue ceramic . . . was a broken cup at harvest tea how many years ago? More balls of twine, and petrol to fill the long oval tank. By evening the last sheaf is stooked and field neat as chess board. Extract a thistle prick — brings blood on thumb, limbs ache, watch swollen sun fall slowly . . . symbolic disc, eye of God behind Love's hill. Head for home, past flittering bats squeak in nettle covered ruin of cottage — Finn said a witch lived in once!

Soon harvest cleared with horse and creaking cart. Sheaves tossed high with pitch forks, building four neat stacks for the thresher — all circus colours — to sort the golden pellets, flow like molten into bags behind. Must be dogs from half the country come. When dark put match to the heap of chaff and watch flames shoot high — is hell like that? Shadows leap and fall . . . some pagan sacrifice . . . was a solemn man standing by the chestnut tree last night?

Can never stand picking King Edwards. Bending to the soil, fingers find the mysterious growers, flesh coloured, touch of magic — once fed the whole country, come whispering words of the hungry years! Try to recall first told about that, they came begging, fever eyed, faint voiced and died by their thousands in ditches. The big land-owner that had nailed to his turnip field gate, 'Take one, take two, but take three and I'll take you!' The Cathedral strikes relief at mid-day, twelve solemn strokes from Downpatrick, its squat square spire on wooded rise above marshes and meandering Quoile river. For dinner eat rabbit and fresh green peas, hear 'His Master's Voice' crackle Schweinfurt, bombings and ball-bearings. . . gives a good feeling to think of dead Germans! On mantel-

4

piece fine framed picture of the red and gold King who gave his name to a potato . . . and isn't there an American cigar?

In the old quarry there is an orchard where wee crabs and mongrel pears grow, rusty reds, lemony and big bitter greens. If one eaten will turn into a toad, as much as one bite does the trick! The place where Finn throws all still-born and diseased pigs; in the whin bushes can sometimes see their rotting purple bodies, moon bodies. Do humans go that way too? Heard them say smelt a ghastly decay and found a month dead constable on the Island in Ballyduggan Lake with no feet! Will always remember that story, how did he get there, where were his feet?

Sunday be good, God wants to see all at Hollymount Church. In a basket seat behind Auntie Annie — like a big flapping bird, pedalling the summery way past abandoned flax mill, Hutton's pub and three cottages of catholics. — Mother's always big, children runny nosed, carry strange beads and never wipe their arses . . . always believed that for some reason or other . . . they piss on the roadside as well! At the silver gates a group of sombre suited men murmur price of beef and eggs, plumpy feathered wives have a week's news to catch up on. Cypresses and gravel path crunch to the little Gothic inspired church completely covered with Virginia creeper. Inside familiar smell of rosemary, only fresh dahlias in two polished brass vases on the altar; cream walls and varnished beams above, flies a sparrow. Three saints in light fused primary colours look down; kneel and pray, the hand of God is close upon one. Sing —

> 'ALONE with none but thee, by God,
>    I journey on my way;
> What need I fear, when thou art near,
>    O King of night and day?
> More safe am I within thy hand,
>    Than if a host did round me stand . . .'

5

Bumble bee flies in the tall lancet window, there is a sudden drumming of rain . . . the sermon ends, and all are blessed.

Spend the afternoon hidden Kelly's bog catching sticklebacks in murky waters with an old silk stocking foot on loop of wire. Fill jam jar tied with a grip string. This place of trembling earth oozing black — sound of punctured lungs! What secrets the sighing bullrushes bending? The body of a perfectly preserved man, hoard of gold or pot of thousand year old butter! Grandfather found a Great Elk antler once, nailed it to the barn door; Finn saw a moving bluish light one night — a German spy! In the long grass there are dandelions and water buttercups, glad sounding names meadow rue, helleborine, cornflower and cowslip. A mallard's feather floats, hare bounds from underfoot; lie flat and watch wisps of cloud drift across, to England perhaps, will have to go there someday when the war is over they say. Warm breeze, half asleep tumble images and fears . . . look up at motionless, mailed Norman Knight. Black and terrible eyed!

And always the brooding Mournes where ever one goes in County Down. A back cloth of changing blues on the little fields and drumlines, a fairy land, world that is both small and enormous.

Walking out to low tide at Tyrella the gulls seem to warn you'll never pass this way again! The long sweep of grey beach and rising dunes is completely deserted. St John's lighthouse is beginning to beam its revolving rod of light — say it's only a paraffin lamp magnified three hundred and seventy-five thousand times. At Ardglass watch the fishing boats come in, from the high pier wall can just see the Isle of Man — where the Ostmen came to fight Strongbow. Is only a line of twenty odd grave men standing shoulder to shoulder into the mist . . .

The trees are nearly all bare, mornings there is frost, Admiral Tovey has sunk the Bismarck, Germans in retreat from

Moscow . . . watching Finn ease nature in a ditch. Same time every morning, bowels move like clockwork, pick him the biggest dock leaves; pushing hard — such a vulnerable sight, lonely, ridiculous really, perhaps the Lord has a strange sense of humour. Harry Hanrahan was born crooked as a hawthorn tree; there's a boy in the town with a pointed head! Vile sausage lumps steam in the cold air, pulls up his trousers and slips braces on, heart goes out to him — a wiry bird with the bluest eyes, could never fool Finn — 'Render therefore to Caesar, the things that are Caesar's, and to God the things that are God's'. Can tell stories that would freeze the blood. Planter blood, swirling blood in an Orange pipe band; he'd practise the strange instrument wailing over fields as would proudly march behind — could face anything with a sound like that, to hell and back, whole German army or Fenian mob! Shoot rabbits at nearly a mile, knows exactly where to wait for flight of geese, is another kind of music the banging of his guns. Bargaining over horses or cattle face grows hard — carved from granite . . . he is Moses, Micha, Isaiah!

The breadman calls with his painted wagon, opens double doors at back and slides the long drawers out whiffs fresh and sweet, rakes currant buns topped with cherries, soda and wheaten bread for mother arms filling. Money jangles through thick leather satchel, gives a sticky something and he is gone brightly, threading the green. Munching it top the big crossroads stone . . . can see the old beggarman from Kerry coming, comes every year; imagine all the way from Kerry and back . . . outlandish world!

Then it snows, old shoes covered from Newry to Belfast, where will the beggars go? Willie Smith found dead in his cottage hear them say from downstairs. So still in the half lit bedroom a strange glow, coloured candle-wax. Awareness of change, out of bed to the window, earth is transformed. Stare enchanted, make drawings on the frosted pane, a ferocious banshee for Finn — will like that! But this morning brings pain,

7

pain that knows it's slowly slipping, snow . . . childhood . . . savour each moment, cushioned footsteps deep, robin on barbed wire, could only catch this day and keep, passes like the wind and rain. Hungry sheep and cattle stare numb, gathered by pump and frozen water tank for hay and crushed barley. Slieve Croob behind de Lacey's racked tower lies lead and barren hard — surface of a different planet, bathed in filtered green gold light, the sun is a circle of silver.

Christmas brings a lawnmower, HMS Indus, wee mouse and letter from a father don't know. Was he in Burma, Italy or North Africa? Mother said when he comes back we'll be off across the water; what will England be like? Say the King and Queen are very nice, King and Queen of Ulster too! The same flag flies, except in the impoverished South of course . . . but England isn't Ireland, in the brain a worm of worry moves.

Ireland's winter bury one, old Willie was a Dublin Fusilier, fought the terrible Boers in Africa, often showed his wound, would be bones by now. Then Matty Larkin shoulder high leads a long dark line from the Cathedral, in January they go; old folks weak hearts — doesn't take much this weather. Never get your feet wet, wear woolly vests and a pair of good thick socks. Cold noses in Downpatrick on market day. 'Touch o' the fluke this lot'. Flogging the poor beasts stumbling through.

Wham!

Wham!

Packed tight in tubular steel pens, look sad eyed, resigned to be meat — carved to little pieces on a hundred different tables. Shoo away dogs sniffing at hens hanging upside down in bunches of threes. Can just see Hannah Moohan pour cold beer between wedged caps, and later Finn's breath is sour.

Soon after Easter the whin blooms brightest yellow on new green fields, cuckoo calls . . . Christ was crucified for you and me! Newborn lambs stumble on rubber legs, poke mothers sore with milk. On warm Spring day walk alone up Johnny's Hill — view Mournes and Dundrum Bay; May Daly waves from her half door, a chirpy stick. Picture of the Pope in there, makes one think, think about Rome — seat of iniquity and sin — said Finn! At Ballynoe Station the red eyed gate is shut to let the blackcurrant coloured train rush past thundering metal on metal in a cloud of coal smelling smoke to Newcastle. Turn right a rutty lane leads to the stone circle, a black goat grazes on the centre mound, three circles of grey stone surround.

Were sabre toothed tigers and wolves about? The huge and slow moving that drowned in bogs. Came a short stunted people that worshipped the moon — gave the tall standing stones a weird smiling face at night, seemed to whisper 'Fools, fools'. Clusters of wooden huts, long funnels of smoke rise slowly in the still air from land covered in thick forest, streams slash, pour to dark loughs where greedy pikes wait, large as pigs. Curling mists swirl, half images, gods made from iron in tall pointed hats; circles, crescents of gold and twisted silver on dark haired women combing each other's hair. On rise a huge curved bronze horn is blown, booms loud . . . soon men emerge in groups, painted grey with metal parts, begin to kill by axe and sword, shrieking. . . monkey like . . . frantically rips at rib cage and tears still pulsing heart, dripping fingers stuff mouth and swallows greedily, gives another man's strength. Soon the rock tumbled place is raw meat. River turns to blood, ravens swoop, hand moves, groans . . . they have all gone, nothing remains, nothing but the stones. There is complete silence, even the black goat has gone.

In King John's field there are tinkers again, evictions'ghosts about begging a shilling or two, left shoe, old coat or stale loaf of bread. Mothers bare footed, have young-old faces, stinking shawls around babies that have no tears. 'Bless ye for half a sixpence, half a sixpence . . .' Voices like soft moaning wind, are shadows, people from nowhere. Say the men-folk have minds of roosters, milk cows by moonlight, would take away and turn into a cripple! Evenings argue around a sparking wet wood-fire — flickers a distorted matt haired, mud hovelled people from

9

Pullabeard's day. Mother catches one flogging a donkey for no reason at all, in a temper breaks his stick and buys for pound. And donkey is ours, seen it all, suffering, knows dog eats dog here. 'Fear not, daughter of Zion, behold, your King is coming, sitting on an ass's colt!'

Get a small cart made by blacksmith McGrath — smokes a Woodbine right down to his lips, nods 'Aye'. Hardly speaks a sentence, secrets well kept . . . making guns for the IRA his light is on all hours! Moves like a bear, sooty low, arms so long can touch his knees while standing upright, can knock out a full grown pig with fist — a sledgehammer! Cottage in scrib land, front is graveyard of rusting dismembered things metal. Inside a dark cavern, glowing coals pumped brilliant by noisy bellows, walls of horse shoes. On heap of coal lie two greyhounds — any thinner and their bones will break through. The half wit brother Shag mutters incomprehensible, searching through a trunk of all sorts of nuts and bolts.

Paint it orange lead and lordly like Caesar, Cuchulain go forth the fields dreaming, dreaming and dreaming all things possible in Ireland. A half painted purple black sky pouring rain and sun shining fantastic gilded view, rainbow curves from the old slate quarry to hollow of rock and blackthorn-blooms, another pot of gold. Cattle like fat insects move across the horizon of Love's big sloping field. By long hedge and forgotten lane slowly wind the way to Bridge' Malle — is a Catholic, but good sort! Lives alone in a cottage that would look deserted but for the smoking chimney. Husband Paddy long dead, drunk into the Quoile, found a mile down river from Downpatrick stuck in the flood gates. Never shed a tear; was it not the will of God for beating her most nights? In the opinion of Auntie Annie. Eldest boy Harry killed at Dunkirk, defending the retreat. Then Pat a year later with the Inniskilling Fusiliers, machine gunned in half with a posthumous VC, she has pinned on S. MARIA DE PERPETUO SUCCURSU, weep not, and inwardly shudder! On a sideboard between two orangy nosed

Staffordshire dogs their photographs fade sienna. A kettle boils on a cracked No 8 cast-iron Stanley Range.

Kind witch, fairy-godmother, has a tin of peggy's leg and stories to tell, with not much to spread on slice of soda bread. Saw the Prince of Wales in Dublin once, 'He was a real man!' And waves the bread knife at the voice of Lord Haw Haw. Was drawn through the city with fine horses and carriage, streets garlanded with paper flowers, the Union Jack flew! Imagine a regiment in red marching down Sackville street.

'Oh those soldiers!'

'There's many the fine gentleman called on me!' She says with a sigh, and a strange beauty for a moment, hard and sparkling. She is not an old woman — young again, gay, wild . . . forbidden! But then they all went to France, rebels burnt the city down, raised a new flag, and her world changed. Hardly understand really except that Dublin is synonymous with Berlin, crawling with Nazi spies, something unsavoury, un-nameable about the place . . . a pot of Fenians, priests, poor begging unwashed, old, falling down, disloyal, dishonest, drunken, lazy, corrupt, stab-in-the-back, people praying to a huge plaster painted Virgin Mary!

And of course De Valera as well — the one man Finn could shoot like a dog!

Bridge' then came North to work for Lord Dundrum at Tullamore House. Made his breakfast every morning — never varied of a hard boiled egg well done, on the floor, ceiling a Bacchic scene; she had to leave, and Harry was just like his father — no mistaking the blood. But husband Paddy somehow knew, she accepted so quick. The hushed words like a puzzle slowly fit together, and the big house still standing, but only a burnt out shell. Place where crows nest, sheep and cattle graze on forgotten lawns, the sweeping avenue barely visible now from once proud pillars lean. Earth takes it all again!

Butcher McGuinness calls with bag of cold sharpened knives, flee fearing to furthest field ears blocked cotton wool; the day

11

is long, mother calling . . . return peek bravely into byre, gutters their blood, bodies hanging emptied, headless on beams. Will never eat meat again, death is a possibility! Supper Finn has fresh organs with toast; it takes nerve to do that!

Morning that's magic wake to find fields covered in strips of silver paper, then parachutes like crumpled mushrooms; down Johnny's Hill count one hundred monstrous Sherman tanks — big white stars on olive green.

The US Cavalry have come!

Sinister long barrels and awful cleaking tread, men with big black ears wave to the frightened boy, 'Hi there!' Can see them crawl like a huge and dreadful worm to Downpatrick. Day and night they come and go, cracks soon appear in the end room walls, the picture of great grandfather in his sash falls, whole house perhaps if the war goes on much longer. A camp of Nissen huts by the racecourse too; Finn says they'll make good hen houses when the show is over, cheap! Like their tin hats, and uniforms much smarter than our Ballykinlar boys. The girls about have gone silly, dream invaded . . . what does LST 1009 mean? Evening closing the hens in step on something — flares greeny yellow.

'My Godfathers!' Shouts mother.

The black faced soldiers surround, ready to kill with their chubby automatics and . . . laughs, offer mother Lucky Strike — smells different in the late evening air. They seem like gentle giants beneath it all, wouldn't hurt a fly; wonder will they be tough enough for the steely hearted Huns? The Captain says he's from New York — where the buildings touch the sky, father came from Mullingar. Always wanted to see Ireland, the twilights are full of memories, knowing, unknowing to North Africa, Normandy . . . most nights half asleep can hear the last post played faintly.

Mr Churchill is plump and prettily dressed as an Air-Commodore; FDR looks very ill, and Joseph Stalin wears lovely boots with a fine long overcoat. The Allies are over the

Rhine and Russians not far from Berlin. All earnestly hope they'll catch Hitler alive, display him in a cage through the streets of Belfast! Rumour has it he'll flee to the South, 'For you couldn't trust them an inch,' some say, 'could just see old Dev and the Bishops greeting him with open arms, installing the whole gang in a fine house in Merrion Square!'

'Would be entitled to bomb Dublin in an event like that.' Finn reasons!

Mother most anxious for the Royal Mailman — nothing now for nearly two weeks from the photographed father — has a fantastic hat and medals on his chest, the nearing day . . . a leaving soon! Then Auntie Annie's victory cake baked back in '39, left behind the parlour couch in a big Inglis tin ageing ripe for all these years is cut, tastes moist and rich. Never thought the day would come — VE.

Too soon.

Making pea pod boats held open by broken matchsticks in the wee wash-house — whitewashed every spring inside and smelling of Dettol. Pour water from the big jug into the pink floral wash basin underneath the mahogany table. They float rather well, could make a whole fleet, have sea battles down in Kelly's bog! On a little carved shelf lie Finn's leather strop, pen knife for castrating pigs (squeals would waken the dead again) and cut throat razor. Sundays watch the reflected face stretched slow and careful, no nicks before Cathedral — collecting the money cushioned by purple cloth on a big brass plate. His head bob bobbing to the altar, bows by the carved stall of The Right Honourable, William Arthur Adrian Percy Ponsonby Godolphin Rumbull Trumbull Prendergast Dill! Will get more pea pods, try runner beans, matches as well — find mother . . . kissing a man at the front gate!

The world stands completely still!

It must be father!

The red ring on the hardware calendar is to-day of course. Sounds English as well, the thoughts run, run to the back

plantation is a cave full of pine needles will hide . . . getting
dark and God only knows what's about. Will have to go
back . . . then England next week!

Think Finn will be fetching the cows home now, at the
station on melancholy mustard walls the big clock moves,
tears, whistle blows flag falls, lurch forward, again; Auntie
Annie waving, slowly out over the marshes gaining speed.
Downpatrick disappears behind the hill of Bones — Danes'
bones Finn used to say by the barrow load, found a skull with
rusted iron through the top helping the Dean dig once.
At Great Victoria Street Station ULSTER IS BRITISH and
stomach an iron ball. In taxi to the docks through the murky
magnificent city, follow polished rails and trams — make noise
like bacon slicers. Huge horses pull four wheels of beer barrels,
bags of coal; outside the Crown Liquor Saloon a man is being
sick. In Donegall Square stark white and part sooty Queen
Victoria holds the world anglicised in her chubby little hand,
the starlings are attacking the City Hall. All the bicycles ever
made from Harland and Wolff's over the Queen's Bridge, come
a rioting river of old sows up Oxford Street, would be English
sausages in the morning would imagine. Can just see the grey
yellow water, reflected lights and fat red funnels, read
GLASGOW HOLYHEAD LIVERPOOL . . . dear God! Inside
high and windy sheds are stacked wooden crates, rolls of
barbed wire, pipes, ploughs, dangerous green bottles in straw
. . . and queues of patient sad people, a woman in tears clings
to her husband, baby roars, an RUC man arms folded looks on.
M.V. Ulster Prince — portholes glow, difficult with baggage
up the narrow springy gangway, wouldn't like to fall into that
lot below. Warm belly of ship is soft whites and varnished
woods, dull thuds, and clean little cabins — drink glass of
water. Stroll on deck before bed, look down to stern end and
third class . . . Catholics, a night to forget, men drinking
already, the poor souls! Decks deserted, different sound —

14

hardly aware of the ship moving . . . Belfast slowly slips, line of tiny lights, stars, could never swim ashore now! The Down coastline is bathed in moonlight and tears . . . dreaming of Ireland!

Over sea of golden wheat a phalanx of luminous green combines slowly snarled. Eyes half closed earth and sky were turning liquid, pouring to the maddened sun; surely the last day would be like this, the final wrath of burnt up atoms, burst of the dying star before eternal night.

Unborn!

And there for a moment — moment as long as all time flashed the ambulance and police car on line of melting metal road. The noise and sight of both faintly registered in the brain of Max Lauder turning the nearest combine: he was racing against time to get as much of the hard red winter wheat cut as possible before the weather turned to hail as forecast.

He could quite clearly see a half naked female beckoning, calling on, leaving nothing in doubt! The attendant lying feet up on the other bunk was engrossed in *Playboy,* quite unaware of his gaze he slowly turns the pages to more delights — looked at different angles; June was blonde in part pinky satin. And he begins to laugh, laugh at such sights on the way to morgue . . . maybe!

But the pain stabbed wicked and deep — felt the soft inner machinery shudder, whole body shake. The attendant quickly got up 'Take it easy boy, we'll soon be there'. He adjusted the blanket, patted the pillow, 'You're gonna be OK now, just shut your eyes and relax, take it easy'. He knew might be relaxing forever, and wondered just what the thirty odd years were about.

That early morning Liverpool — could cry again all day. Dockers have the strangest accents, city sort of grime upon grey with no green hills and fields in the distance; what a place for the third class passengers to die! Bodies will float, lie putrefied on muddy Mersey banks — swilling shamrock eyes. The English put Irish flesh in their pies, mix it with the old sows so one wouldn't know! Ovens of Irish well baked — Belsens! A plate of Paddy with shamrock sauce is a good filling meal! Mix Irish blood with their oil — lasts longer! Use everything but his shouts — think up a use for would make a fortune! Silly ideas flood, for can't be all that bad, remember father's English, was nice to bring those toys and German medals; fought the war together and Ulster's part of England too! A whole night's journey away now, how many miles of sea? Would be picking early morning mushrooms this time, place by the bottomless well were beginning to grow.

Mighty Midlands — heart of England's wealth, workshops of the Empire, everything from a nail to steamroller one flat. Factories of fearful machines — steel clawed up and down, faster like an automatic guillotine the rhythm never stops. In streets of slums children play football. Pointed mountains of coal, turning spoked wheels on legs, tall chimneys spew sulphurous clouds — hang like damp and dirty blankets above.

There are houses everywhere.

At Birmingham Mr Atlee smiles.

The land is very flat . . . Leighton Buzzard is a monstrous bird; the home of Cadbury's Milk Chocolate, and Spearmint Chewing Gum; to rest in a great Cathedral of trains. Irish voices quickly lost . . . then sliding doors (would cut in two), racing red underground; lifted by slotted stairs, the people are like drab wax statues, up up to the pale sunlight and acres of ruins. A very different kind of world. Such soldiers on horseback in blue and polished steel clatter into the fog . . . faint chance had the ancient Irish against the ancestors of these. Can just make out a rich quartered flag high above Buckingham Palace.

17

Would the King and Queen know we left Belfast last night?

To big house of high windows, Indian brasses, ornate furniture inlaid with ivory and dark oriental patterned carpets meet an English grandfather. Very yellow with terrible face that seems to be only half there, is strapped by waist and legs to a wheel-chair.

Man or monster?

Stares blankly and has to be fed by bottles and tubes. He suddenly raises his only arm at intrusion and shouts, 'Charge the buggers!' Then wheeled off in disgrace by a little ferret like man who calls him Major. Father says he's an Old Contemptible — one of the first to fight the Kaiser's grey hordes. Recognise his photograph — very athletic looking with long sideburns and upturned moustache, there is a bearskin and big buttons, 'Second Battalion Coldstream Guards, Aldershot 1912'. In a glass case are six medals, behind the King's head one reads 'For the Preservation of Civilization'. Another shows Victory crushing Hun symbols. Drink tea and eat buttered muffins . . . sort of gurgling sound comes from the next room; on the opposing wall is a huge print of the Duke of Wellington's funeral. Crossed Ghurka knives above every door, can hardly sleep for thoughts of the staring Buddha.

Early light wake to an ear shattering 'PREESEEEENT ARMS!'

Then September sadly brings an English boarding school. Enormous pile of red Victorian Gothic, pointed towers, high hammer-beam roofs, gold and black Roman clocks that strike every quarter across acres of quadrangles and playing fields.

Through the big wrought iron gates of St Oswald's — arms a molineux cross, motto 'Not afraid to die for my country', in a new blazer and striped cap wave to parents and reluctantly go. Hang around the big studded Junior school door a bit, feeling noticed and not wanting to go inside, told to go outside, then inside again . . . and by two marched to supper. How grand

18

the Bishop of Lichfield looks eating roast beef with the head-master and senior staff on raised platform above two rows of long tables in the great hall. Hooked nose and white hair rather too long, a silver pectoral cross shines on his purple shirt, looks every inch an English Protestant Bishop — Latimer or Cranmer! Most boys seem so keen, stuffing the main course with gallons of sweet tea and bread, all sorts of cakes, buns, biscuits, crack-ers, jams, jellies and potted meats produced from special boxes and tins kept in cupboards at the end of each table. Talk about colours and teams and who's going to play in what and where, there's a wog in Lower Third, Coates was having it off with Smithers last summer and O God keep eating and hoping they'll not notice too much, maybe run away and see if could get to Liverpool and . . . the bell rings, Bishop says prayer in Latin.

Another by the Junior Housemaster, each kneeling before his bed. Lights out gaze at stars so bright in the inky nothing; be best part of the day this, free to travel in dreams far from here — could never fit in, will have to leave, just simply get up and go. Very quietly does it, mustn't wake the others, cold, ten shillings safe, few sweets; strikes two thirty climbing through the bootroom window, not a single light on, stick to the main roads first, will make for Chester. Morning God only knows, seem to be in Wales. Chirk a pretty little place, fine castle — lived in as well. Llangollen ten miles, why not try for Anglesey and Holyhead have boats to Belfast, or do they only go to Dublin? That might be risky, Finn wouldn't want to meet there, better ask the way to Liverpool . . . was biggest mistake ever made!

Monitor Mellowes is delighted with task to bring before headmaster, knocks smiling 'You'll be crippled for the rest of term after this!'

'Enter.'

Looks up from paperwork behind his desk red faced, bald and one eared.

'I've heard all about you boy, this sort of behaviour just

isn't good enough! What would your father think? An officer with a distinguished war record, son running away, afraid to fight the battle of life. What? St Oswald's doesn't tolerate that kind of nonsense you know, and when we strike we can strike very hard!'

Leans back and from what looks like a huge spent brass shell case draws a long bamboo cane, bends it to and fro.

'Got to learn to play the game by our rules now, nobody's run away in years; we have a great tradition, tradition that won't be broken! Many a fine old boy from here . . . Sir Arthur Morrison-Bell, General Hamilton KCB MC, Admiral Sir Reggie Skelton . . . ' He puts down the cane for a moment and counts the long names on his fingers. '. . . remember little Pimm MC at your age, a plucky little devil, popular as ice cream, would never turn from a fight . . . now bend down and take your punishment like a man!'

Stinging pain rips backside six times . . . dance out the room; will be marked for life by this, in the Junior School changing room they're waiting like harpies ready for some dreadful sport, expertly led by Jones III and Brown V.

'That'll teach you to run away you blubbering little drip!' Says Brown V.

A mob of wicked young faces surround, shoot pellets from tubes, jab with little pins, detect a strange accent . . . from Ireland!

'A Paddy!' Says Jones III.

'A Paddy!' In loud chorus.

'You helped Hitler in the war and your parents live in a pig sty, will have to punish severely for that!' Shouts Brown V triumphantly.

Sobbingly try to explain that Ulster's an integral part of the United Kingdom, fought on England's side during both wars, Churchill thanked for that, Jerry bombed Belfast as well as London and father fought too, has a gold and blue passport reads 'UNITED KINGDOM OF GREAT BRITAIN AND

NORTHERN IRELAND'. There is a difference, not Catholic Irish but Protestant — pledge allegiance every Twelfth of July, the Governor, ROYAL Ulster Constabulary, Sir Edward Carson, Craigavon, Somme, like Wales or Scotland, English as Yorkshire, take after the father usually — English as they. Know Land of Hope and Glory, God Save the King by heart . . . but it doesn't do any good, they've never heard of Ulster before!

Imagine!

Brown V in a thick accent, 'Where's Ulster Paddy Pig, where's your bag of potatoes?'

The mocking laughter, will be known now as Paddy Pig — object of fun and ridicule: they'll never understand the difference, don't want to know, perhaps the South was right!

Such a thought!

As head pushed down the lavatory and flushed. From the door Junior Housemaster has been watching all the time, seems delighted with the sight; could go out and die like the elephants when old. Underneath a full moon at Ballynoe, simply fade away not a trace!

But mother says will have to stay on, learn to be British! Would rather be Irish, Ulster anyway!

And O so slowly the novelty of baiting Paddy gradually wears off as each year brings a fresh crop to choose from.

Singing carols in the candlelit chapel, choir dressed in long red and white robes, boys are briefly transformed to angels. In the soft glow can barely read the golden words carved in marble above rows of names —

They shall grow not old, as we that are left grow old:
Age shall not weary them, nor the years condemn.
At the going down of the sun and in the morning
We will remember them.

With old Mr Sylvanas very kindly a bit of extra history some spare afternoons. He smokes oval cigarettes and sips sherry from a cracked tea cup. Room sour smelling, pillow-slip of unwashed clothes, mean bar of heat, books rise from the floor. Poor man looks like a scarecrow, gown torn and turned to sort of constabulary green, throws his butt into potty from half under bed, fizzles dead. Walls covered in team photographs . . . and Luther's hammer ringing out the change. Puts the kettle on, remembers a bag of gingerbread men matron baked on top of wardrobe. Biting off head he says with a grin, 'I like eating Boys!' Chats on a bit, thumbs through the fresh printed —

S.D. Waterworth, who has completed his second year Birmingham, was awarded a scholarship by I.C.I. at the end of his first year.

The Rev. J.M. Oak (1926 — '30) is Vicar of Finchley.

Boagey
Bray
Cameron
Coates
Edwards
Elphick . . .

'And Hartly had a peculiar smell . . . in Singapore'. He mutters.

We congratulate P.S. Horn . . .

Events have proved again that sustained House and team efforts reap great rewards . . .

GAMES . . .

Grief was obviously in his element as the villain of the piece . . .

Over his shoulder from the cold little fifth floor cell can see that Shropshire is covered in thick frost, a few people are skating in Colemere. Counting the weeks to August and holidays in

Ireland again, last year on top of Slieve Donard, below like a living map and Duffy's Circus all red and yellow toys just outside Newcastle . . .

Returning, churning slow up Belfast Lough between orange buoys in a chilly morning breeze. Undoubtedly the best time of year with a whole four weeks ahead in Ireland. Great skeletons of ships rise on the south side, noise of steel on steel, fat gulls glide, swoop and 'gah-gah'. Cave Hill is bold and clear in the dove pink sky. Can see people on the quayside waiting. recognizing and waving; accents hit like cold water, butter milk . . . almost forgot with a smile, will get used to again, it's good to be back. Father's Austin A40 is lifted from the hold.

## GOVERNOR WELCOMES PRINCESS

Be launching some ship or the likes, around hospital or old folks home, all those Union Jacks; what will wee Meg make of Belfast? There's a mountain of soda bread, bacon, eggs and strong tea waiting from mother's sister of the Newtownards Road.

And O such a fuss for Bridget the maid from Donegal has left with all Bertie's pyjamas. Her underwear and 'Well we just aren't sure what's missing yet.'

When returned from weekend at Portstewart she'd gone.

'And after all you'd done for her indeed, isn't it just typical of them!' Says mother.

'Well, it'll be a lesson, never again' Replies aunt.

'The little slut, could hardly speak the language when she first came.' Mother goes on.

'If I ever catch her I'll, well I'll . . . ' Fumes Bertie.

And know fine well father's trying hard not to laugh.

'Wasn't it a family of ten, my God they probably wouldn't know what pyjamas are for.'

Bridget was pretty, and well, well she shouldn't have stolen . . . can do what they like really are forgiven at confession.

Most dreadful deeds, anything . . . was always Finn's reasoning!

Is over the fields with scythe cutting headrigs to let the binder in. He doesn't see in the ripe acres like Father Time the swinging shoulder and arms slicing rhythm, solitary, strong, all knowing — such an uncle to have! Poppies this year, the many points are like cornelians set in rich gold.

'Holy Moses boy you must have grown a foot!' He greets.

There's a family of fieldmice underneath his peaked cap in the stubble which dog has been warned not to touch. Pikes are biting well along the marshes, frog cut from a crepe sole shoe does the trick grand, this evening. Foxes in the back plantation, quarry orchard a hive of bees in the body of a dead pig; two horses sold and new grey Ferguson attached to the cart has small rubber wheels now. On down a bit to Kelly's bog on dragonfly's wings hovering polished blue and green: land is warm, air sweet and heavy, glutted cows munch, swish tails, so beautiful to see all this now. Sudden realization of life, body filled with light — seeing for the first time, past and present brought to this point, splitting seconds, alive and conscious piercing deep . . . could die this afternoon and no one need mourn!

Will definitely go over the Border this time, can only just re-member the last in a hotel during the war when a man got up and drank a toast to Hitler. Mother broke her cup and silently cursed, for father any minute could be killed fighting the mon-ster. Even offered condolences to the German Ambassador when Hitler died! Finn raved for days about that and now warns 'Mind your step across there and watch the Fenians don't get you!'

Is he joking or not?

Newry to Dundalk, rising bit mountainy, look back to Down is so many little hills. Our Customs man waves through, heart pounding a tatty green shed.

STAD  STOP

That flag, and there painted on the rock side. Lighting a

cigarette ambles out, peer proficiently slothful eyes, un-crowned harp on cap and buttons, uniform dirty and sausage fingers on the car door, has rotten teeth.

We are in Eire — is a foreign country!

Dundalk early Sunday — milling masses, overweight priest pink faced in shiny black suit, post box painted deadly green over crown and royal monogram — the blighters! Boys with no shoes on their feet, little mite can hardly be four asking for pennies, a dog with three legs chasing his tail, the pubs are be-ginning to fill. Drogheda peer at barbarically hideous Blessed Oliver Plunkett's head in a glass case at St Peter's R.C. church... the natives of Borneo keep relics like that. Mother thinks it's disgusting! Little candles burning at feet of Mary the Goddess, a young girl prays — long red hair flows to waist, lips barely move, crosses herself, walks out dancing eyes, sprinkles with holy water . . . indeed, didn't Bridge' keep a prussian blue Milk of Magnesia bottle of the stuff from Lourdes to rub her arthritis with?

And O Dublin!

Fenian capital! Smells of turf and coffee, gazing up the Liffey from O'Connell Bridge in a daze and gently flowing high green water and rosy buildings . . . unreal city, dreamlike with no definition. Nothing to catch hold of, it disappears when reached for, floats, past the shuddering drunk lying flat on his back with a bottle of Guinness in each hand. The GPO and bullet marks in the columns can see and dear God it must be the IRA. That agitated young man yelling hoarse about the Six Counties, others selling the *United Irishman*, have a sort of half mad look, eyes that could kill perhaps! Girl in ill fitting clothes with them is a face from the last century — suffered and fervid beauty, hands out pamphlets to passers by. Mother swerves with an icy stare, says it's 'The seat of treachery, where the great stab in the back began!' Felt so ashamed as a girl that Easter week, especially as eldest brother William was fighting in France. Looks up at Nelson, 'At least they left him alone!'

There's a sad and forced gaiety along O'Connell Street. Parnell Square and Municipal Art Gallery — is one large painting of the funeral of Michael Collins, coffin draped in the tri-colour . . . those colours, rebel colours, catholic, Irish blood everywhere. Was Finn Irish? Yes. No, he hated everything that flag stood for. Yet; yet he was hardly British, English. Father was English. Perhaps a seed of something begins to grow, who knows, was English or Irish?

Does it matter?

Heart in this island without a doubt, Ulster certainly; but can one live in Ireland, or is it just a place of childhood memories and holidays? Could claim an Irish passport, born in Ireland, mother Irish — as Irish as any down here, were all in the same boat before partition. Could hardly imagine Finn in England, be like a fish out of water, yet he knows all the loyal tunes, is King William most years! Who'd want to be governed by a state run by priests, a hold on everything, better to be British really makes sense . . . yet father going soft for it, even talks of retiring to it — makes the brain disintegrate read somewhere!

On Grafton Street woman is playing huge harp who blesses father when he puts a shilling in her cap. The melancholy playing follows nearly up to St Stephen's Green, late evening sun fingers golden the great squares casting shadows and soft lights. From the hotel window at the back can see gaunt someone very carefully picking through dustbins and filling a brown paper bag. Finn said they were starving! Downstairs murmur of voices, warm fire, polished brass and faded things; three priests having wine with their meal, is that proper, should priests have wine with their meals? Chew chew, laugh and light cigarettes . . . in this Fenian heart, asleep . . . kissing red headed catholic girls!

Phoenix Park and the Zoo are almost deserted, slowly the long straight road through stately parkland, a fine white house and galloping horses, dreaming, the distant smoky mountains, low painted pillows of passing clouds.

Sign to the Papal Nuncio's Residence . . . the tentacle of Rome!

Can feel touch of autumn the first leaves are blown, whole country holding, transfixed this numbness creeps, which way? The great finger of stone points to heaven . . . few tiny figures trick about the base, before total destruction!

Buy peggy's leg and Sweet Afton, for Finn a pipe carved into a grinning leprechaun smiles 'Top o' the morning to you'.

Second week to Glenties, Donegal. The Ulster Bank, rear to cobblestone yard, high arched stables turf stacked, assorted cumbersomes and vegetable garden to rock strewn rushing after heavy rain river Owenea. With clumping waders, dressed in army surplus, tweed hat coloured with own made flies, fine cane rod, gaff and net uncle William the bank manager never seemed to mind them — patient and concentrated ties a fly . . . and casts beautifully. Moving on a bit to pools knowingly and a different fly is more times than not rewarded child with rod bending would snap to courageous trout or salmon — leaping trail of diamonds in the glorious afternoon. River runs to Ardara and Loughros More Bay, lazily along the banks watching him, thinking of nothing in particular the day, piddling on a curious shaped piece of bleached bog oak since Adam and shaking hands with a dead bony tree. There are bats at dusk underneath the bridge dripping green, do the lobsters boiled alive for tea feel pain?

Would wonder why they have a branch at Glenties, so few customers, little for uncle William to do. Away most days around three with gun or rod, quick brave swim at Portnoo — pier into Gweebarra Bay the boatmasts dip and rise, scudding skies emit sudden shafts of brilliant light, dancing tweed colours. World of its own Donegal . . . doomed, ice cut, pushed, planed bare and rock split rolling away to horizons of more rain and God only knows what coming out the mist carved upright; are moon faced angels buried in thistles and ragwort, with the devil well out to the front!

At Port perhaps realise as no other place that who or whatever doesn't give a tinker's fart for man or pigs, gone away, whole village once, just cottage walls, was a vegetable patch, ribs of rotten boat. Strange rounded boulders heap the horseshoe shaped beach part flooded by turf coloured streams, sheer cliffs and monotonous sea pounding the terrible silence . . . could go quickly mad, scream all day and who would hear?

Walking up the valley can just see someone on the highest point watching, can they fly? Gives a faintly uneasy sensation. Where the car is parked by field no bigger than a large room, back hunched like a grotesque wing and rope over is pulling door with six inch nails nailed into makes a harrow up and down forever . . . punishment for some long forgotten sin!

'Work n' fit for a beast!' He shouts.

They're digging turf in long blackish rows — heads at ground level, in knitted cap waves laughingly and swigs tea from a narrow green bottle, has a nose that would do well anywhere! Coming down to Glencolumbkille is covered in thick fog, the protestant church tower penetrates to weird effect. Mysterious place of what dark secrets kept beneath the damp layers hidden? Vague and ghost like hurry along from what must have been a funeral, in weather like this. Hates Churchill's guts from inside McShane's pub very slurred, sheep wander through the village, an old woman peers forlorn hands clasped up and down from her door. A grating noise, louder . . . is a wheel barrow of manure, few still at the graveside, priest comes from rear of the chapel and drives away. Wonder who is wearing Bertie's pyjamas?

Then as if by command the sun shafts through, in a few minutes the sea is solid blue with not a cloud coming in. Draw faces on the sandy shore, seagull lands on slab of standing stone — faint cross the new light down in the hollow of whin bushes.

Symbolic of what?

Triumph of time, droppings on the lot of you! Take the path to Glen Head . . . what century tread? Up and up the rocky path meandering over lunar like, eroded from turf cutting down to rock and scattered stones are skulls against acid soil — place of some ancient and holy battle. Could meet a leper, knight or grave man, line of round shielded Celtic warriors . . . but a ragged boy leading donkey with two creels of turf, shyly smiles. So high now sweating, sun, sky, sea and bronze valley after valley could become fused with, the rushing air, dissolved

I am an estuary into the sea.
I am a wave of the ocean.
I am the sound of the sea.
I am a powerful ox.
I am a hawk on a cliff.
I am a dewdrop in the sun.
I am a plant of beauty.
I am a boar for valour.
I am a salmon in a pool.
I am a lake in a plain.
I am the strength of art . . .

Terrified, faint, blood lost, aware of all this and self burning . . . is too much on top of the world. There is a black tower on the cliff edge which from a distance looks like an empty iron mask.

Awful feeling again, like knowing will die this week over, catch all now and store, hold for another year. Alone watching Paddy Curran slightly drunk with mongrel dog, on his bicycle meandering the narrow way bursting a thousand different greens, totally unaware — everything as it should be, pockets stuffed with the *Down Recorder* and long brown paper wrapped packet. Sees and stops, dog a quick pee, strikes Swift match to his pipe and mutters, 'Be off across the water soon suppose?'

How it hurts to be reminded, just wandering from field to field going nowhere, the pain . . . that day in Dublin — not so bad really, strangely foreign, yet . . . South a sort of yesterday land, old photograph come to life, hardly touched by this century seems, strange quality of time standing still. Dublin sinking under the Liffey, drive for miles without seeing a soul, the neglected acres, mad wide villages with heart gone, big silent houses behind trees. Nature in Ireland never much disturbed simply taking over again; catholic religion perhaps — not this world but the next that matters, God will provide, pray hard enough . . . the poor fools!

Deserted yet the past breathes so heavy, dead walk wherever one goes. View, old bit of ruin, carving or such can trigger them off . . . those tiny men in line with sharpened stakes around a blue hill from Donegal to Pettigo! Country holds like a vice, away always the yearning to go back, will never leave alone, like some terrible disease — insidiously corrodes and destroys all hope of a sensible life. Like to go back and live after school, doing what? Could hardly work in the South, what would Finn think — relatives? Queen's University — haven't the brains; what and where in Ulster is going to be a problem.

Paddington Station again early September feeling drained, indifferent and blank to the whole ritual of going back to school. The pimplefaced boys in long scarves and trunks piled on the platform. Few carriages 'St Oswald's only' corner by the window watch the dreary scenes flash past, and compare to last week in Ireland . . . with those Dublin girls very nice, more so forbidden fruit, kiss a catholic they'd die!

Awakened at Crewe, could weep, can see Barton striding far ahead with soft leather bag and hockey stick can't wait to get back, be a prefect this year suppose, will do very well for himself no doubt. In the bus from village to school they all start singing together, and quite suddenly feel very Irish — green Irish! Will definitely go back to live there.

30

Paint in thick posters a full ripe marigold moon above Legananny Doleman — coffin shaped blue black, thick strokes of olive earth, face from otherworld — if only you knew! Slash Slemish Mountain like a great breast in a screaming sky tossed birds, the cripple who looked like a monster spider limping sideways down that Donegal pathway. Angels are bats with fly eyes about the tumbled abbey, those dole men holding up walls the Catholic Repository Downpatrick. Huge heads, barrel bodies, dwarf feet, line upon line of them. Reflected greeny pale sky in water, the silence broken only by church bells; could paint all day would let you. To live for each hour, Viking like and all before thirty dead on a County Down shore, heart transfixed by black iron and cold beauty.

The VB boys sit listless and daft as chickens, gaze out the lead paned window, afternoon classes drag by. There's an Irish girl working in the kitchens can see most times filling the big metal urn with tea. Whole senior school be after her — won't stand a chance, be done a Sunday walk the woods about Colemere. Nice looking too the poor thing, happens nearly every year they have to leave, then Head before the whole senior school about smut and the carnal desires. A giant suspender belt hangs in the great hall, in carved oak — house arms of swans heads eating treble crosses; he takes off his sellotaped horn rims and wipes clear with inside of shirt front, holds them up to the light and continues reading.

Speech day comes the Countess of Cavan in a big Humber Pullman to distribute the prizes and speech. Flowery hat, pink chiffon and fat pearls, perhaps she'll do a little dance and lift up her skirt to the rousing cheers, goes on and on about the dear school and how well everyone has done with altogether eighteen boys leaving who have obtained university places including four at Oxford and Cambridge . . . to the day when school will produce its first Prime Minister!

And then the great news, father's resigning from the Service

31

and going to try his hand at the pigs. Assured profits reckons
Finn building a new subsidized piggery most years now. Could
go to the Belfast College of Art if wanted or become a farmer
and live in Ireland . . .

From far off satellite the blue and white planet earth reflected brilliant in the black infinity. Faint greeny brown was all that showed of the North American continent. West across the Atlantic Ocean was fading into night, turning away from the sun it would be late evening in Ireland now, the first stars appearing over scenes he knew so well. Ireland not even a green prick from space, dissolving into the darkness, Europe and swirling low cloud masses. Lights be lit for a while then one by one turned off as the whole island took to bed, faded into sleep and those magic hours between midnight and dawn. Rich and poor alike, birds be roosting, furry creatures deep in warm burrows, dogs in kitchens and cats wherever, isn't it only the owls and cows that fly at night?

And where the satellite passed like a strange silvery insect earth was really rather insignificant, a dirty golf ball, speck of dust in the immensity of time and space, what was important, what really did matter? Was his life, life in the balance, a delicate scales poised on the highway to Kansas City so soon? Heart was beginning to beat irregular but the brain was still very clear.

That first view of Ballylaneen near Ballynahinch, two gradual hills of forty-nine Irish acres, one field exact centre of County Down. West is Slieve Croob, south the Mournes, from highest hill facing north-east pale Mull of Galloway across

33

from the Ards Peninsula. Belfast is fourteen miles north as the crow flies, night a faintly acid glow in the sky. From winding road a short avenue of ivy choked elms leads to Ballylaneen — long, low and sturdily built Plantation style with very thick walls white-washed and bottoms tarred. Slate roofs from a square yard, back of which is corrugated iron hayshed painted bright orange lead by flax hole where water-hens flit, make delicate traceries in the mud. To the front of the house on a freshly painted flag pole the Union Jack flies. Neat garden of raspberries, black and red currants, gooseberries, plums, tomatoes and apples. From end bedroom window view the gently contorted ground rising to long mountain that turns purple in summer. Sixteen fields in all divided by thick hawthorn hedges; between the two hills runs small stream, awake at nights is music under the wee stone bridge in Ulster's heart beating softly, now could say was living in Ireland never to leave, no dates to worry about or holidays quickly slipping.

Area considered good protestant land that mustn't be sold to the Romans that bid two or three thousand pounds more! Sad widow Coulter couldn't live about for doing the likes of that; there's more in a military rank and cousin who's got the Down High School badge on his cap — gold on green reads right and the farm is father's. Says that some of the money paid will go to build a lodge extension in memory of her dear Jack, be in new amber brick with rosewood doors and enamelled brass panel!

First thing father does is lower the flag and saw up pole for firewood. Brings mutterings abroad, but what can they say, say to an Englishman who fought all through the war, has a good rank and a Military Cross? Mother is rather upset and says the wood makes sparks that burn holes in the carpet.

And now the elation of a real home in Ireland, rare drug taken — old sheepdog Shep left behind can talk and even dance with the moon his eyes turn to little darting lights as explore all hours together. Mysterious chair of stone, blocked up tunnel to where? Highest hill remains kind of circular dwelling and six ancient sycamore trees. By stream a place completely closed in by whin bushes and rock, sit for hours drawing, watch as evening brings the long slanting shadows, green turning dark, enormous hares grazing, clouds of gnats, olive buns of cow dung, simple wild roses, and dog lying completely contented his new found friend. Another Union Jack by crossroads far off is like a bright flame or blood on the dissolving landscape.

First year let half the farm to Dogherty brothers Jimmy, Patrick and John. Bachelors live with their invalid mother in a three roomed shack up towards the mountain and poor ground where the chapel is! Go in to see with father, family sitting around the fire on egg boxes and two old bus seats, my God! Baby chicks under lamp in tea chest chirping, room smells of sweat, tobacco and paraffin. The Trinity adored by the Heavenly Choir. Over the fire a big black pot, side goose wings for ash dusters. Have a sort of gypsy look, like big gaunt birds, could even say aristocratic the sharp noses, ancient chieftains, Kings. Call father Sir, and seem rather touched would come in and drink their tea. Keep near five hundred horny black faced sheep between them, owning no land have to rent. Price is agreed to of ten pounds an acre will pay and leaving they all see to gate, mother wheeled, watch the car disappear.

Can see them coming slowly by the lake, they look like scarecrows on bicycles front and rear the wool bleating confusion to big twin gates — open and wait, glide through like a shoal of fish and spread out hungrily stripping the fresh grass. Jimmy slides the bar through and fondly contemplates his flock, fixes with hazel eyes and says, 'They'll do well there rest a th' summer.'

'Aye.'

'Aye.'

Agree others, light cigarettes, spit in puddle of water by thick honeysuckle — crushed in the hand smells of long ago . . .

> My lady is a prety on,
> A prety, prety, pretyon,
> My lady is a prety on
> As ever I saw

Week passes they're up to something, mischievous gathered, queueing takes turns through a gap in the hedge, have to hurry and chase back, with slasher cut branches and fill. Counting them most days the late summer fields, a four leafed clover, wish . . . Road below is like a ribbon of violet around lake and Ballymack Presbyterian church, sky thick with crows very high going straight like black knights to war, priests elect a bishop perhaps, Pope!

Dusk, a promise of winter and Shep running ahead some ferocious creodant carnivores about his brain, sniffs here and there, stops, listens and frantically digs, the long lost ancestor maybe! What images race, killing and blood wet through dark forests after, in packs howling to the moon. Two figures from Fitzmaurice's closing pub pass, mumble 'G'night'. To a lonely death, rising higher, by Dogherty's and through lit window can see Patrick earnestly cleaning wax from his ear with a match. McGoogan's quarry a grey and reddish veined wall, bit looks like a face, filling his lorry rattle bones with long shovel stops and waves, at this hour! How he makes a living wouldn't know. Job here and there a few quid, handy with the dynamite removing those rocks for father, big smile drilling the holes and pushing down the grey sticks.

'Ah sure 'tis amazing stuff!'

Maybe was he blew the B Special hall up. Awoke the whole neighbourhood . . . and is a catholic too!

The ministry pine plantation is a hushed house of the unknown, wind gently in the tops, and behind the long mountain Slieve Croob since time began a risen harsh shape like great stranded whale, a falling star momentarily. Road runs out, not even a bush now, can see Dundrum Bay bathed in moonlight, St John's lighthouse flash its warning, remember grandmother telling how her mother used to pray for the souls of poor mariners a wild, tempestuous night.

> Bitter is the wind tonight
> It tosses the ocean's white hair
> To-night I fear not the fierce warriors of Norway
> Coursing the Irish Sea.

Lights of Belfast, Ballynahinch and Downpatrick, only sound is trickle of water, tastes mineral, ice cold. Neighbours be talking these wanderings, suppose are sort of settlers really in their eyes, even mother away for so long considered English . . . pagan and untrustworthy! Pray for their salvation from the devil, Westminster and Rome; way looked at in church last Sunday that business of the flag no doubt. Sorry for new clergyman from the South ringing the bell on St Peter's Day, were waiting at the gate with pitchforks and crow bars! In no uncertain terms never again, St Peter was the first Pope! Even Finn seems different now . . . things he says sometimes.

As the dawn begins to hint, thick mist in places dissolves all shapes away, there is dew on a million spider webs, every nerve receiving existence that hurts as can't even begin to understand the mystery. Two swans sweep low and land in the lake behind thick reeds, church clock strikes five, open the iron gate and look at the names — Patterson, Savage, Love . . . Door is unlocked slowly up to the altar never fails to move, this awful silent, sublime and completely indifferent God, could take communion now and His Son would be there to intervene. Stand up to the eagle lectern and read —

> Remember now thy Creator in the days of thy youth:
> While the evil days come not,
> Nor the years draw nigh when thou shalt say, I have no

pleasure in them;
While the sun,
   Or the light,
   Or the moon,
   Or the stars,
Be not darkened,
Nor the clouds return after rain:

In the days when the keepers of the house shall tremble,
And the strong men shall bow themselves,
And the grinders cease because they are few,
And those that look out of the windows be darkened,
And the doors shall be shut in the streets,
When the sound of the grinding is low,
And he shall rise up at the voice of the bird,
And all the daughters of music shall be brought low;
Also when they shall be afraid of that which is high,
   And fears shall be in the way,
   And the almond tree shall flourish,
   And the grasshopper shall be a burden,
   And desire shall fail:
Because man goeth to his long home,
And the mourners go about the streets:

   Or ever the silver cord be loosed,
   Or the golden bowl be broken,
   Or the pitcher be broken at the fountain,
   Or the wheel broken at the cistern.

   Then shall the dust return to the earth as it was
   And the spirit shall return unto God who gave it.

Vanity of vanities, saith the preacher: All is vanity.

Dog nervously peering up aisle.

Stock the farm with sheep and cattle, Finn will help — an

38

expert's eye for good boned beast to grow plenty of meat means money and His favour above!

Allam's sales yards Belfast then, the pious and canny Ulster farmers all shades of dull, nod, knowing their business, language — mysterious monotone of prices and good buys. Auction ring thick smoke and rapt attention auctioneer's tripping words, sold to an invisible hand and pigs skiddle through, chased by boy in oversized coat with knotty stick. For Finn the day is more fun than Christmas, his ten fat cattle fetch a good price, will buy father a bottle of stout the way home.

Fifty Suffolk sheep bought and six young bullocks loaded into the Ulster Transport. Leaving see the Governor driven in a big Austin Princess — from cushioned depths lifts faint hand at few.

'Bloody old fool!' Says father.

'Ah now I can't agree there. He's our link with the Crown, embodies all Ulster stands for, the Queen's representative. A reminder to Dublin that Ulster is British!' Finn replies.

'Hmmm' Murmurs father.

Can't understand why he won't join the Orange Order and vote for Brian Faulkner as well!

There is silence until get to Carryduff — where Finn mentions his mind on a fine new Spanish style house — all white and green slates would like to get the plans of and tear down the old home — would make good foundations.

Reservoir's full, fresh from the Silent Valley and know his surely unreasonable fear of an insidious IRA mentioned once unloading drums of arsenic into by night and poisoning the protestants of Belfast . . . every stomach be seized by maddening pain and all Ireland would be lost! Thinks should be guarded by armed soldiers twenty-four hours a day.

The ram gets busy and does it so quick, Finn says 'If ye haven't a good ram ye've damn all!'

For he's now married a good protestant girl from Ardglass, played badminton together the church hall, eyes met through

39

net and that was that. Baby William was born last year, roared
his devils out . . . or in . . . at Hollymount church above the
old Norman font — that was buried for five hundred years.

Without really knowing then or much thought the end of it
all, College Square and Belfast's Municipal College of Technology — great mass of sugar white Edwardian baroque, highest floor the Art school. Apprehensive up the many marble
stairs, arctic walls and rows of tall metal lockers, stained glass
windows — the industries of Ulster. Small folder of work —
how will it compare? The first year students in groups about
all seem to know each other, those accents that self righteously
proclaim. Brings a vision —

WHO SAID WE'RE TO HAVE HOME RULE?

COME TO BELFAST AND WE'LL SHOW 'EM

Solemn whiskered men grouped around a round table
Union Jack covered, sign —

> Being convinced in our consciences that Home Rule
> would be disastrous to the material well being of Ulster
> as well as of the whole of Ireland, subversive of our civil
> and religious freedom, destructive of our citizenship and
> perilous to the unity of the Empire . . .

Trying to draw an Emperor's head, white-washed figure
throwing the discus, filthy ditty pencilled on his backside. An
awful lot of students doing art, where will they all go, get
jobs? Girls be married early enough — cut the number in half,
rest teach suppose, few make the grade at this or that. Could
one sell enough paintings to live? Make pottery, silver jewellery
perhaps . . . in Ireland? Definitely the answer as to what to
do, yet there's something disquieting at the back of it all. An
unrelated world high above the reality of Belfast. End is a long
way off though, will surely take care of itself . . . she has the

loveliest knees from pink flowery slip just showing have ever seen exactly opposite.

Chairs U-shaped round a goose fleshed girl nervous in the raw. Small breasts and sloping belly, rather too bony, catholic face the almond shaped eyes and long dark hair, small cross from a delicate chain . . . is all Ireland in those deep peaty pools, pools of pain? Comes hard pencilled pointing and murmuring about form. 'The maximum with the minimum amount of effort.'

With a few deft strokes brings to life beside own stiff and sausage like, hands and feet are shapeless sponges, face an unrelated mass. Could nearly weep at those drawings of Leonardo and John.

Chrysanthemums in milk bottles or pinned to boards. Rusty, yellow and white showy many petalled head, grey green wave edged leaves to lines . . . much easier than life. A single red rose, rather well really.

A weary hour of Roman lettering reads CONSUBSTANTI-ATION painfully with sable hair brush and black ink. Composition's figures are like sacks of stuffed straw — reel over the Boyne Bridge to some unknown fate down Sandy Row. Modelling dull clay — primeval lumps moist from a hinged wooden bin; standing by tall tables with narrow spaced legs and swivel tops. Pluck little bits to start seated man and woman. Beside now she is faint perfumed, has tiny mole on her high cheek bone, look that could cut in two, wouldn't do to make a wrong move.

Michelangelo's David stares over, and out into the swirling depths — growing dim, fog covering Belfast, the ABC Cinema looms ghost of the Titanic! Just about make out —

## STAND FAST IN THE LORD

Lockers bang and corridors empty, Donegall Square's a rush of hurrying home, she dissolves into Bedford street . . . lost forever, in the Ulster Hall . . . some fearful sacrifice!

41

At Ballynahinch think George Warren looks slightly mad at his pumps filling a Land Rover. Croob Park is very neat the well kept gardens and lawns, red, white and blue painted kerb stones. Left King Billy's way past the Earl of Seaforde's big hay field. Generously most years the Orangemen can march to, gather and hear speeches from draped lorries . . . bowler hatted nod, the warnings of a devious Republic conspiring for reunification, IRA planning to obliterate the Border by armed force.

Rage!

Rage!

Ulster achieving great things through thrifty industry and sturdy good sense, the low standards of democracy and justice in Roman Catholic countries . . . Same field as the Battle of Ballynahinch was fought. Acre or so of Celtic wood, the huge chestnut tree is the colour of burnished gold, shaft of sunlight the hawthorn berries — are drops of blood. Comes the Earl's daughter on a mahogany horse, tight fitting tweed and twill up and down, doesn't even notice, dog after.

Shitty bitch!

With that book on early Irish metalwork . . . Ardagh chalice, Tara brooch and those strange shaped pieces . . . the day behind Finn ploughing bog field, unearthed a twisted sort of wire, then another, curious took them home and roared loudly when mother made give to the old gentleman from Ulster Museum for half a crown — threw in the fire! Month later up to Belfast, and cleaned — matt yellow and rich, from County Down BC something. Said the Irish were great metalworkers once. Mined in the mountains of Wicklow, wrought to moon shaped collars and clasps, interlacing patterns and scrolls; something unearthly their remains, from what dead planet came? Drank blood and honey, hunted wild boar the dark hills, inky lakes . . . and now Rafferty, Stewart and another, hardly aware have begun to learn the ancient and mysterious craft.

A stony path to where?

Difficult and slow, peaning flat circles of gilding metal on dished tree stump with ball faced hammer; then bowl at an angle on straight metal stake, raise the sides in from the centre with blunt wedged hammer singing. Raising turns the metal hard — softened by annealing to cherry red with blow torch on table hearth spinning. Let cool slightly then plunge in cold water, dry in sawdust and ready to work again. True the bottom on a flat top stake, gradually arriving at a cylinder shaped piece. File the rim even, planish smooth with polished round hammer. Solder thick wire on the base, boiled clean in sulphuric acid and water; to the lathe with special compounds and mops polish gleaming . . . the mists of times are gathering.

Working late, three extra classes of craft every week. There's time to fill from five to seven, the coffee is strong and creamy in wee cafe across from Technology building — main door gather, in the cold, as if nowhere to go.

Is despair here?

The wind torn clouds race, reflect city's lights . . . ghostly echo to leave! Rafferty roars past on his ancient BSA. Girl looking slightly ridiculous in duffle coat, red stockings and stiletto heeled grips tightly behind, the direction of King Street.

Sips coffee slowly, dander back and in early, soon lost to the magic craft, silver's brilliant lustre, soft glow, mysterious mirror of reflected shapes and light . . . will walk her up the Malone Road to grandmother's the week days. Just in time, chance the same direction she thinks, another cup of coffee at the Piccolo.

'That would be nice.'

Her eyes are candleglow, lets hold hand beneath the minute table. Sucks cubes of sugar from rough earthenware bowl, talk of nothing really until must go. The streets are deserted, sort of smoke pale haze, two fantastic shadows keep rising and disappearing from the gaslights, lips taste of sugar a darkened doorway. If only there was somewhere to go . . . University Street so soon, her grandmother be waiting the grey two

43

storied with huge brass head knocker, lights on, eye at the window — curtain falls.

Eye of God!

If ye live after the flesh, ye shall die:
but if ye through the Spirit do
mortify the deeds of the body,
ye shall live.

Angel face walking two grues . . . 41 lace curtains, 43 asleep or dead, 45 lemon glow and National Anthem, 47 gently turn the long key. Mustn't wake Sarah Coogan up, three flights of complaining stairs, attic room smells damp and moth balls . . . the skylight window is cracked. Beginning to rain and think all Ireland is a grave.

<pre>
        I
        R
        E
I R E L A N D
        A
        N
        D
</pre>

Hand in her hand along the Lagan sketching boats and grotesque willows. Back row the News and Cartoons, nipple rising between thumb and forefinger . . . emerge half blinded; fool to attempt monumental effort of the Northern Bank with its great central hall lit by glazed clerestory windows. Playing a mournful saw between his knees, buy her a posy of violets in Donegall Square, thinks daft to do and little bag of heart shaped sweeties — munch for lunch the lawns around City Hall in the sun. Couple of HB's Erskine Mayne and afternoon assemble composition from morning's work.

And as much as can manage the craft have chosen. A fantasy world of whatever, piercing angels in chorus around a bangle. Phantom, pagan deity, knight and man of grave vision; mitred

44

bishop, king, queen and foetus faces stare, bodies of pinky sliced tourmaline. Bird across a gold washed moon, old woman praying, Finn sowing the corn seed, Adam and Eve, Daniel in the den of lions, heaven, hell, man and woman embrace, laughter and sadness, birth and death, all life in a piece of jewellery. Don't take too seriously. Engrave on a silver pendant in thick uneven letters —

> I am of Irlaunde,
> Ant of the holy londe
> Of Irlande.
> Gode sire, pray I thee,
> For of saynte Charite,
> Come ant daunce wyt me
> In Irlaunde.

Ireland, in Ireland a silversmith!

Belfast — who'd buy? Jewellery the best bet with odd commission of holloware. Few hundred quid be enough to get started . . . where? Couldn't afford the larger towns, have to be somewhere small, near enough to Belfast . . . or Dublin . . . perish the thought!

But why not?

Small workshop and front for tourists, well as selling to shops in Dublin. Say things are picking up down South since Lemass took over; read something other day about grants as well.

Easter thumb ride with her to Dublin, doesn't really want to go; through Newry in a cattle lorry cramped, beside stout and thick suited manure stained joker.

And pang of uncertainty again, into an alien land, whiff of incense, strange rites, unknown, ridiculous really, will never leave . . . yet not English . . . Irish . . . cursed! Border kind of no man's land, reedy, scrubby grass and stunted bog trees. Some fields away a bright stone cross catches the sun, and know a man died there fighting for Ireland . . . his country!

Can feel her regret at coming, the ghastly ride, smell of cattle for weeks and dumped in the middle of Dublin, never even been to before!

Carry her duffle bag, sullenly beside into Frederick Street and down O'Connell. It is cold and the city thrusts upon, by the pillar she slips gold plated silver ring on annoyed and somewhere, anywhere . . . find a room in Abbey Street seems clean enough, but strong suspicion sheets haven't been washed . . . 'Dirty Irish!' Says. Suddenly bursts into tears and bolts the door.

Small sitting-room downstairs sit to the dying turf fire, smell reminds of Donegal. Nothing worse than woman sobbing, unreasonable, should have stayed at home. Girl at the desk keeps looking at, heard the crying probably, very old man shouts for correct time, must be stone deaf, slowly sets his gold pocket watch. Time, time running out and hungry, go buy chocolate covered biscuits, apples and milk.

Chance it now, the door is unlocked, she is fast asleep — under the sheets sort of curled like a baby sucking thumb, at eighteen, the auburn confusion and lacey patterns. Open the roll of biscuits, drink from the bottle, draw the dirty curtains, turn the lights out . . . there is Irish music and laughter . . . drifting.

. . . in Dublin . . . Dublin . . . dirty Dublin, dirty Dublin is sweet . . . rich faded brocade, old ladies and pastry faced boys, on a bottle of stout up the Liffey . . . in love with her perhaps . . . all Catholic and wicked wanton dragging unto . . . in Dublin, Dublin . . . there isn't an honest man left now . . .

Through the window sunlight streams universe of floating dust, true grimy state of room, but mornings always hope, and try to remember the dream. She is up and dressed — daisies on blue, sits on bed earnestly applying holly red lipstick, touch of this and that from little snapping discs. Her mood has passed, sees awake and smiles . . . and know, know that she will grow old and die and be forgotten, but it will not have been in vain, for today, this morning, in this shabby room off Abbey Street, sitting on the tossed bed, legs crossed, toilet finished, she is Maggie — so young and presbyterian from Cullybackey, born for these eyes to see, in the casting of a stone on bogwater.

It is Good Friday morning and O'Connell Street is nearly deserted, summer coming early this year. Sprawled underneath the GPO, alive or dead? Over the bridge, a canopy of pale blue and high whispy clouds, rowing down river in bowler hat, vest and small black boat disappears below. Gulls glide lazily — as if nowhere to go. Many flags flying look rather beautiful — pale soft colours, Fenian colours, colours of sacrifice, blood red Christ nailed on Calvary. Shed so they might live, wash sin away and make men free, from Rome, the British! Blood the drink of Church and State . . . enter the Trinity.

Opens a gracious world, and slowly each cobblestone quadrangle, the lawns and classical facades. The great Long Room library is strangely open — dark and silent, smelling of church, pedestals and busts, aged browns on billiard table green these hushed hearts to modestly displayed in a glass topped stand the Books of Kells and arm around her waist.

Christi autem generatio . . . The never ending rain, carved mountain out of barrenscape, swelling sea's His breath, the fearful eye of light, make ever glorious each passing day, death His will, the greying geese are souls of dissolute priests.

Pray.

Pray.

Morning noon and night — a great full moon slowly ascends the Celtic vision of Christ crowned resplendent of every colour adoring, their madness endemic, entwined, from starving bellies, genitals, damp celled the flickering oil lamp sways the finger of Satan everywhere to chase . . . and fall screaming the fierce cliffs and headlands, windswept bays. Their rapt gaze, absolute belief, would calm the wildest beasts and cruel hearts for a life and death brawl about cattle or the likes. Patiently each twist and turn, will go blind such work, crouched, constipated, can't think for a drop of it, was her soft white breast revealed a sin . . .

Madness on every page, foot in other world, sort of grotesque cleverness, their God gruff schoolmaster in the sky can strike like lightning, but occasionally smiles and forgives if genuinely sorry. And the Devil never far with his fork and bag of doomed souls. Make a bracelet of fallen souls — just faces slit eyes and pinched mouths . . . a diamond studded Seraphim.

Circle of Saints.

Dancing priests.

Virtues and Vices finely woven around her finger.

Lifts and tolls away . . . kiss by doorway — no one is looking, and up to Grafton Street. From West's to Switzer's to Brown Thomas looks — can have whatever she wants today money is no object, perhaps the ornate gold and amethyst brooch from Louis Wine, they're all closed. World its own Grafton Street, across to Stephen's Green — trees beginning to show their new colours, lie on the grass . . . birds twitter away . . . would be nice . . . workshop in Dublin, Wicklow maybe; whatever it is that pulls towards this place — dreamy and sad and childhood's terrors. Ducks and pigeons waddle near, she tickles with a leaf . . .

The few days race; crowded dance hall sweating rock, electric music deafens, girls dressed to the nines along one wall, watching, waiting, tarty catholic are capable of anything given the chance! Actually see de Valera — like a wise old crow, comical almost, the steel rimmed glasses on hard beak, in dark suit on stand in O'Connell Street watching the military parade. Second rate army, something from World War I, Collins's murderers, shot soldiers in their beds . . . yet strikes that again within. Plaque to Michael Malone killed in action April 26th 1916. Walk the whole length of Phoenix Park and hold her behind the thickest trunked trees. St Patrick's

Cathedral gloomy and dirty banners, train to Dun Laoghaire and Bray — windy and deserted, can see the Sugar Loaf mountain. Laughter's too loud in the National Museum . . . spinning fantasies those shapes the othermen wrought to sail away from Ireland in tiny paper thin boats! Names Lunula and Pennannular, simple shaped cup, Ardagh chalice bold and sure the fine bands and bright studs, long forgotten lips would touch the spirit of God. St Patrick's bell . . . ringing clear . . . same steps as Finn's surely, are rows and rows of gold crosses on red. Saint's arm, tooth, foot and crozier. The bones of St Manchan, Bogman and Viking cries — 'No! No! There is nothing after death!'

Huge trumpets and cauldrons of bronze, graceful shaped swords and axe heads, wooden shields, golden discs and hollow balls — what strange purpose? In busy workshops ringing, bent and bad tempered, would cut off your nose if looked sideways at. For the King in his hall, making love and war, bawling and treacherous, great bear of a man simply gouged out the bound prisoners' eyes and crunched underfoot. Playing chess by firelight and growing old, herding pigs and cattle, making butter and cheese, drinking milk and mead, listening to the harp played melancholy. Hunting man and beast, watch the raven high, sun set and moon rise. Along some deserted shore . . . never knowing why: the highcrosses of stone, crude box of alderwood that kept her jewellery, same cupped ending shape she wore.

Dark or fair?

Laughter that filled the world, tears and lovely face reflected in clear flowing water. Half naked children playing, a cape of undyed wool and one leather shoe. Long ships with dragon heads and black sails slowly in packs, wolf packs into the wide estuary . . . burning.

## GOD BLESS IRELAND

The blood stained vest of Connolly, rules of Irish Republican Brotherhood, faded flag of plough and stars, rusted revolver and dead patriots' uniforms. The Proclamation and reflexes the villains' names — Clarke, McDiarmada, Pearse . . . Last letters before execution, yellowing photographs of marching men . . . all gone in the oceans of time — mindless and still. The two big rooms are empty of people, not a sound can be heard.

Drink Guinness and eat salmon between wholemeal, the pub is crowded, they sit on tall stools, by low tables, ordering another round the words spew forth . . . this fascinating bit read in *Time* about Piranha — can strip a body clean in less than five minutes! Aren't they a slick bunch, crunching an onion chip, burps back of his hand and offers Afton . . . think he is a free man but his grandfather wasn't . . . and all the dead past reels and stretches from here now — drinking his pint.

Oblivious!

Unfold the new map of Wicklow, awkward, see . . . Enniskerry be handy the city, Roundwood, Delgany, Glendalough perhaps . . . the awful doubts! Mountains Mullaghcleevaun, Lugnaquillia and Djouce. The Vale of Avoca, into Wexford, Carlow and even Kilkenny. Will come down next year again, try to settle the year after.

She's playing her harp the corner of Grafton and Duke Street, the last sixpence for luck and both are blessed in Dublin again.

McCoomb's bread van will take her from Ballynahinch to Belfast. Willie Rogers lifts half way to Ballylaneen on his battered Ferguson, sit on bags of meal built around back axle and drawbar; expresses amazement at having been to Dublin.

'Sure 'tis run by the Bishops and they're leaving like rats from a sinking ship!'

Explain otherwise he grunts, 'Ah now!'

Squeeze past Rafferty stupid drunk and vomiting down the stairs that leads to a room and dying party. Step into the early Belfast morning — it is clear and promises to be a fine day. She wasn't there, hardly blame her really, with a silversmith messing down South of all things; as her grandmother would say, you can't live on love, without money it goes out the door!

Hurts though wandering over to his bike and kicking alive; Stewart bleary eyed passes with a huge paper bag of something over his shoulder suddenly tears pouring empty beer bottles that shatter and roll into the Lisburn Road everywhere.

Speeding machine exhilarates, sets free, half way between life and death, to Downpatrick and trying to remember who last night said, 'We're cursed by the past, cannot change or participate in the present and will be gone tomorrow!'

Downpatrick the ancient county seat, people been living here for nearly five thousand years they say, the great fortress mound at back of the Cathedral. Look at grandparents' grave, crows harsh cries echo in the tall trees above. Can just make out in the distance Finn's new pighouses, he must be making a fortune! The Cathedral is cool inside, hymn numbers set and things polished ready for tomorrow's Sunday services. Sitting in his pew with goggles and crash helmet in lap is a shiny skull! Think is here would want to be buried, place of birth, where bones will lie forever in an Irish graveyard.

Past still there waiting for miracles and God only knows what the Catholic Repository and Town Hall the dead vacant stares — all hope gone their fag ending days a dark shadow to Rea's Milk Bar and an ice cream.

She can't be more than about sixteen sipping frothy coffee through a straw and sitting alone the empty tables. Like a saucy child, too much make up and short hair streaked blonde and probably from Irishtown! Upturned nose and tiny mouth, skirt too short reveals a very nice leg, absentmindedly says 'Isn't it terrible warm?'

Buy her another coffee, she smells peppermint, and quite unashamedly asks for a spin.

And why not?

Take the Newcastle Road and dear God the skirt is nearly up to her waist, make a detour of Finn's! Grips tight, rests the side of her head on shoulder — nice that, overtake the East Downshire coal lorry into Clough with its wee half tower and flag flying brilliant against the clear sky. Can see the sea glinting into Dundrum, army targets of Ballykinlar across stretches of shallow water, sand and coarse grass. Narrow town and right, up to the Castle, massive broken walls on gracious stepped and rocky ground. Shady trees are like great fans. Still sitting on the motorcycle she lights a cigarette and blows the smoke straight up in the air. Offers one — last one from a crumpled ten Players pack. Slides off back, hooks arm in arm, 'That was super, now let's go inside the Castle.'

Strangers yet she's completely uninhibited, as if known for years, through the narrow pointed entrance climb the winding stairs in the wall.

'Oh it's dark in here, protect me from the dead!' She says half jokingly.

Arms around then the winding passages push together, stop at each arrow slit to view, fourth kissing, and out on to the flat round roof spinning. Both gaze leaning on the big warm grey stones, sun blazing directly over Dundrum Bay — dancing gold, silver and diamonds, the looming hazy Mournes, and the green green land . . . hold a million years in circle of fingers, could stretch out now and rub away the memory of Ireland.

Other side the long hump of Slieve Croob. It is nearly midday, she seems in a trance, still gazing doesn't say a word. Wonder what dull witted routine was kept here, the metal-nosed spearman, de Courcy's banner from highest points. She suddenly turns, 'Take me to Newcastle.'

Buy double helping of fish and chips wrapped in the *Recorder,* together on the nearly empty beach slowly demolish the greasy pile. Bare footed run over the wavy ridged sand and wash fingers in the sea. Pick rare pink shell — which she takes from and keeps. Name is Maeve, 'Just Maeve.' And that's all she'll tell.

'Live today you've lived them all.' Laughs and marks weird

little figures in the sand with a dirty comb end.

And think it's only too true in a fatalistic sort of way; catholic reasoning that, give no thought for the morrow, for the morrow takes care of itself isn't it? Hands circle neck and pixie eyes fix, 'You're nice you know.' Kisses slowly . . . with Maggie it was never like this.

Brake at the deep rutted lane to Tyrella beach and Mad Dog stream ending. Race the long beach splashing and her laughter infecting, a wide and fast turn where rocks rise, can see the drunken line of tyres in and out of the sea. To the dunes and tall grass that hides, lie and kiss again and again . . . fall asleep fitfully head on her lap . . . canting seagulls, sun still hot and high, it is mid-summer's day the 22nd of June. On bellies part grasses together, watch the few well scattered cars, people tossing a rainbow ball and ridiculously small dog dancing. Old faded railway carriages on both sides that make summer homes, always wondered how they got them there. Place where Finn thought it a disgrace for one selling ice cream on a Sunday; and pitied the poor soul for the wrath to come! Could just about make it through that gap, no one would notice a swim in one's underpants.

Waiflike on the rise she waves, lonely figure, blows a kiss, and back, she is the only girl in the whole world. Would last forever, into the cold water, deeper deeper, taste salt and she still watching . . . waving. Curious seals bob beside, bark and disappear. Ride each wave slowly rises and falls to Earth's motion, dive a greeny blur . . . what's it all about? Tide must be on the turn, watch that, someone drowned last year, most years; Brunel's Great Britain in 1846 lay all winter. Grand-mother's grandmother used to tell her about that, into the worst famine year! Father brought the whole family down to see the iron wonder. Must be nearly tea time, run back to her, pats dry with cardigan, 'Don't mind, it's falling to pieces anyway.'

'Maeve.'

The sky is turning buttery pink to blood over Donard, hardly any darkness at all these nights. Could have something at Finn's — look aghast at Maeve, the tarty little . . . just about enough money for petrol and something that wee place at Ardglass. Skin tingling salt and grit of sand, bike hums the sweeping road, warm evening, too many flies, through Killough and Ardglass just tea, bread and homemade strawberry jam. And sadness creeps, walk along the pier . . . getting very late.

The fishing boats leave — soon just a line of dipping lights into the Irish Sea. It is ten o'clock, and all a pale lemony glow, moonless and first stars appearing, few shadowy figures. Holding her so soft, vulnerable, lines of tears streak make up, be as pretty without it. Last embrace so tight, tight, inhale sweat and cheap something . . . O little woman, woman, become one, race the heavens together, take and keep, another memory . . . of Ireland!

Downpatrick the pubs are emptying, leave at Market Street, lewd whistles and words gaping lads, cannot kiss now . . . last glimpse she looking back, and then gone, gone forever into Irish Street!

Run out of petrol just leaving Seaford climb the scrubby hill by lake, startled sheep huddle together, at the very top stand and cry out loud.

'God!'

'God!'

He doesn't answer, there is complete and utter silence, a frightening silence over the sleeping land!

The ambulance was slowing down he felt, weaving in and out. Screech of brakes and stop. Tyres squealing — off again, the big Cadillac ambulance was like a huge and soft springy bed. Always liked American cars, so roomy and reliable, never gave any trouble with so little looking after. Powered this and that, a joy driving the wide endless roads and . . . another sudden stop. Horns blaring, must be nearly there, attendant's face glued to dark tinted window. 'The God damn fools, can't they see it's an ambulance!'

And that inner trembling again, quite violent this time as if soul was impatient to be free, break away from flesh and bone . . . be so far away . . . and once more his mind leaps that great distance . . .

In the pouring rain drive all over South East Ireland trying to find a place to set up. Enniskerry and Delgany are too expensive and dear God the sombre mountains are like heavy rolling seas; could have gone on to London and well, well there's no going back now. Nothing in Roundwood, Rathdrum or Aughrim. There's a cottage up a lost lane somewhere going cheap, but looks very damp and local warns there's a dispute over last owner's will. Whatever that means, drive on. Into Tinahely and Bunclody a funeral procession . . . make a good brooch that, the gaunt muttering men, box high and priest's robes flapping. Round the Blackstairs Mountains, through

55

Graiguenamanagh and down to Inistioge sick with doubt. The Nore is a raging mud coloured torrent under old bridge, village most attractive set in the valley, and well kept tree lined square. If only the sun would shine, in the Spotted Dog warm to good fire and drink a double brandy. The madness of it really, who on earth will be interested in silver around here; just sink into the mud and be forgotten . . . preserved like the butter!

'Sure isn't it terrible weather we're having Sur!' An old man in long soaked mackintosh and water dripping from his cap bends and rubs claw fingers to the fire.

'Haven't seen the likes for many a year.'

And 'Would ye be from the North Sur?' Car registration probably tells that . . . cunning . . . has a sister up there . . . the conversation drifts along. Worked for the Tighe family as a boy and remembers night the IRA burnt their big house down. 'The blaze could be seen for miles.'

His eyes seem to dance momentarily.

Looks a bit incredulous when tell about plans.

'You wouldn't be serious now would ye?'

Then mentions Mooney. Five miles away, little two storey house in the village opposite the chapel for sale, see Parker and Pearson the Estate Agents, Kilkenny. Buy him another drink. 'Thank ye kindly Sur and good luck!'

The rain has stopped.

Drive a steep hill through pine woods that open out to soft rolling country, distant hills, streams and ruined towers to another valley is Mooney. The sun breaks through descending and village becomes jewelled, and all things are possible now, who'd want to go to London?

Village is three pubs, three shops, ten or so dwelling houses, tiny school and grotesque cement and pebbledashed chapel all clustered together on each side of the narrow road. Directly in front of the chapel is the one for sale. Freshly lime-washed, celestial blue door and biggish windows will give plenty of light, good guttering and roof with two new dormers. Like a

56

doll's house, be just the job. Have work place and shop downstairs, live on top. Can have a sign hanging out, be hardly any alterations at all looking through the windows, a silver haired lady is watching from next door, smiles. Better go and see the agents in Kilkenny first, could stay the night.

The hotel walls are covered in Spy cartoons, hardly altered since late last century seems. A bite of tea in the dining room. Many mirrors reflect pale yellows, creams, dark furniture and polished plate, pair of huge antlers on shields. Next table someone has left the local paper —

## WE KNOW BEFORE ALMIGHTY GOD WE ARE RIGHT

### Did They See A 'Flying Saucer'?

'It stood out against the mountains in the Mullinahoe district and it had either landed or was hoovering over the ground. There was bright lights on the objects and it had all the colours of the rainbow . . .'

### THE 'ABRACADABRA' PRIEST

### Practical Patriotism

### She loves Ireland

## ALPHABET FOR JOY

L is for LOSS. Loss of time. Loss of opportunity to do good. Loss of a chance to answer God's call. And L is for LENT which is a call to make up for all that was lost. If today you hear God's voice do not harden your heart. The time is NOW.

M is for Mary . . .

## STOLE CAR BATTERY

NOONAN —
A heart of gold stopped beating,
Two smiling eyes at rest;
God broke our hearts to prove to us
He only takes the best . . .

Mr P A Macauley (80) Friary Street, Kilkenny whose death occured recently was a founder member of the IRA in Kilkenny and was vice commandent of the Kilkenny Brigade. He was second in command in the attack . . . stirring days of the fight for freedom.

## POLITICAL INDOCTRINATION WARNING TO MACRA

Pioneers Meet in Kilkenny . . . If the wife of an alcoholic goes to visit her in hospital pioneers could be of practical service by offering to baby sit . . . work of the pioneers should be more than spiritual; it should be apostolic work . . . the abuse of alcohol led either to death or complete insanity.

### 'LIKE BEING TRIED FOR OTHERS DOINGS'

### 'Make Country Better for All'

### INCIDENTS ON A BINGO BUS —

. . . He said James O'Hanrahan put out his tongue at him . . . the three of them were fairly drunk.

### 'PRESS CAN HELP CHURCH'

### DEATH TO SCUTCH

### The wedding day is coming

### RAT RACE FOR THE NATIONAL CAKE —

. . . ridiculous that a small creamery with 400 or 500 members should have the same voting rights as the bigger creameries . . . heard one gent say he would kick in their guts . . . fight for Ireland for which Pearse and McDonagh died and for which their fathers and grandfathers fought . . .

Muintir Chief Denounces Scandals

Remand on Theft Charge

DURROW DOINGS ... was drill instructor for the IRA over a wide area ... coffin draped with the Tricolour ...

FINED FOR TAKING SALMON —
'These people are like vultures praying on the helpless salmon.' Waterkeeper Michael Mullins said he caught Cosgrave under the bridge by the sleeve of his coat. Waterkeeper Kevin O'Carrol and John Burke corroborated ...

THE SLAVE MERCHANTS

LOVE AND KISSES

THE PEKING MEDALLION

THE NAKED RUNNER

YOUR LUCKY STARS —
... fairly sure that you are not carrying a spiteful vendetta just to satisfy your ego. There does seem to be ample course for you to be alarmed and angry. Avoid even numbers.

Basketball Girls Prepare

Stole 30s.

Drainage is driving out the geese

An Irish farmworker driven to distraction by flagrant immorality near his bungalow in Dagenham, Essex, decided, with his family to try to clear the area of prostitutes.

Whiskey Theft sentences

NAOI gcead bliaian go ham seo sheas an chead Normannach ar thalamh hEireann. Nil fhois agam an ...

The Rosary on Television?

MONSTER SOCIAL IN WINDGAP

. . . the essential injustice of the whole set up in Northern Ireland.

BARBED WIRE

HANRAHAN'S DAUGHTER

ELASTIC STOCKINGS

BONESETTING

CAPABLE MAN

YOUNG GIRL

RELIABLE

MANGOLDS

30 HENS

DONKEY

SOWS

'Mr Parker won't be long now.' Says the faint spoken girl settling back to her ancient black and gold Underwood. High draughty room, one naked light bulb from cracked ceiling; mountain of books and stretched cobwebs, black tin boxes with names Thankerton, Tollemond . . . Large and ornate gilt framed photograph of the Marquess of Ormonde hangs over the cast-iron fireplace. Door opens to tall and pot bellied dressed in coarse bright tweeds clutching papers.

'Good morning Sir. Now that property's a fine place, was being done up for Charlie Maher but died the day after retired in New York. Terrible tragedy indeed, the Lord moves in strange ways. Indeed he does! The price his widow wants is an even twelve hundred, and of course there'll be fees.'

Settling into his cluttered desk, offers thin Schimmel-penninck. And then silence, even the typing stops . . . could just about make it with help from father. Birds are singing in tiny back garden where a young girl is pegging clothes to a line; can see the battlemented heights of the great Butler castle. Her movements are so graceful, on tip toes leg muscles stretching and she is totally unaware . . .

Finn reckons will have to most careful! 'Why in the Free State of all places man dear?'

Mother puts a brave face on and says it's still not too late to go to London. Father lets have old Austin A40 and with few odds of furniture and tools drive across the Border early morning when Customs be asleep.

Afternoon when arrive, warm and sunny day the dreamy country-side, somniferous air drugs, could go to sleep anytime – does anything really matter? There's a fire going in the sitting room, three yellow roses in a tumbler of water on the window, fresh loaf of bread and jug of milk in the tiny kitchen. Knock on the door brings Maggie Anne – lady from next door.

'Such a fine day to welcome you now, I brought the second key.'

She seems quite excited and places the key on mantelpiece.

'I lit the fire as well to air the rooms out, thought there was a crow's nest in the chimney but it seems to be all right. There's bread and milk in the kitchen now, you'll be wanting to unpack.'

Makes to leave but hovers by the door telling all about poor Charlie Maher.

'Sure I remember him as a boy, left just after the Troubles he did . . .'

Must be well over seventy, her gestures are apologetic, deep lined face is wan, wears red slippers with fluffy white balls, looks comical coming from such skinny black stockinged legs.

61

Finally leaves and start to sort things out. Few figures watch at a distance, children pass giggling; bit unnerving that, but they'll soon get used to suppose. Finished close the door, fill silver cup with milk and break bread with a little cheese. Falling sun fires silver in hand, there are flies trapped on the bubble glass panes. Bread is good, heavy footsteps and figure momentarily darkens, slice of mother's apple pie, peel an orange, wash fingers and lie on the sagging camp bed . . .

Startled to life by clatter of hooves and creaking cart, shouts 'Gahhhan!' See disappearing one end of the village. Dab face with cold tap water and take the Kilkenny road going nowhere. The slow, gentle angled and lazyland without people, clouded sun now gives great shafts of light.

Aureole.

Dew brained and angels lifted this day — in Ireland has made it all worth while. The fleeting moment totally aware, the miracle transcending; wind on wind this evening will never end. Crossroads two boys are pumping water from an ancient pump. At forgotten Kells a jar in the little red and cream Licensed to Sell. One sits to the counter silent, the plain woman behind continues her knitting, clickity click, clickity click . . .

Walk over sheep sloping fields, river's song about, this many towered and walled place. God's ruins, weed blown and ivy tumbled, once proud Augustinian priory more magnificent now though, the thick brambles in towers, be lots of blackberries soon, insects hum. On a toppled arch sit and wonder would their prayers and hymns have reached Him? Lines learnt long ago.

> The earth goes to the earth glittering in gold,
> The earth goes to the earth sooner than it would;
> The earth builds on the earth castles and towers,
> The earth says to the earth — all this is ours.

Moon rise and soft darkness, heavy dew, owls' hunting hours. Drive on, viewer to the magic places, shapes grow and vanish, few living lights; fields of moon are water. An island of trees and Round Tower make harsh silhouettes, fresh cut hay in silver curving rows, gate the rusty bones of a reaper.

Ancient Kilree church, three walls and thick cypresses. Earth pregnant of graves, the Round Tower looks down with a black eye.

Unearthly!

Phantomlike!

Risen sudden from the hedge behind . . . it is a high cross, pale, circle arms, embrace, kiss lips of stone.

The chapel bell wakens a continuous ringing, sounds people outside, men all along front of the house talking in low voices. Going to Mass suppose, an orange Volkswagen drives up and out steps a plump priest, takes final drag from cigarette and flicks away an abandoned soul, quick word with one and hurries to back of the chapel! Will have to get good thick curtains for all the front windows, wouldn't want them all staring in, enough curious glances already, keep low! Interesting shapes and faces, women in their very best, men in dark baggy suits, V necked jerseys and caps, one, two nice looking . . . yes are really in the deep end now, outnumbered, besieged, last one alive . . . they'd have a fit, for goodness sake times are changing surely?

Watch gradually filter in and doors are shut — bottom of which is a mouse hole. Few late remain outside, kneel on one leg . . . can hear their muffled prayers and hymns, wee shaggy dog bold as punch skips up to the chapel wall and pees, sniffs it and skiddles on — to hell with your God and religion!

Over they flood out to shops and Sunday papers. Odd looking character selling the *United Irishman*. Priest hurries away to his big house overlooking the village, can see the bright car drive up to. Some say prayers in the graveyard, others remain in gossiping groups, then into pubs while women wait in cars. Street gradually empties, discarded cigarette packs and sweet wrappers blow about and a cow wanders through.

Sacred Heart of Jesus, blonde and very blue eyed stares slightly askew from end of the bed. Dress take it down, fall dead flies and ear-wig from behind!

And busy month soon slips making house right. Brennan supplies Kosangas for cooking, heating and working metals. Nice bit of olive tintawn for showroom — off-white walls, amber tweed curtains and make four pyramid perspex display cases with tiny spotlights to highlight. Sign over front door and engraved brass plate as well. Word soon passes, 'There's a silversmith in Mooney!'

No name, just the Silversmith.

Drizzling day wondering what first to make, at bench and sheet of silver before. Tractor going far too fast passes the chapel and bouncing youth automatically crosses himself, sort of reflex motion, they all do it! Sexton is digging a grave with three helpers, take turns with the long handled shovel, keeps pausing and bending while others peer down, is it bones they've found? Brennan's head just visible from his shop entrance scans the village up and down, a great nose; Maggie Anne crosses over for something, they go inside. Other window to back sheep are busily grazing, cock heads sideways under wire trying to get at garden's untouched grass. Mite late for school in wellingtons trying hard not to look in. Father Bollard stops and goes over to sexton for a while, then into chapel and soon emerges carrying the Virgin Mary — which he carefully places beside and off again. Where on earth would he be taking her? Always seems to be in a hurry that man. The drizzle turns to rain whipping windows; gravediggers cover the hole with an old beige door and bicycle off. Will the funeral be today or tomorrow?

The Angelus is rung.

Draw four lost figures together from their waists, low line hill behind and sky a strange bird, big round Tiger Eye is the sun or moon. Late afternoon solder hinge and catch on the back, it is ready for assay. Then ring with two heads — happy

64

and sad in just under an hour. After tea Brennan brings a very worn signet-ring that he wants made two sizes larger. Watches fascinated as few quick taps of hammer brings it the right size to slip over his fat knuckle. Give it a quick polish.

'That's amazing the way it comes up.' He enthuses.

Maggie Anne shuffles in and gets a chain untangled, haven't the heart to charge them anything, but he leaves ten shillings pleased as a child. And think that's about all the trade will get around here, will have to build up a range and try to sell to the shops in Dublin. There's only about eighty pounds left on account in Kilkenny!

On a while yet, with a sort of figure like Brennan saying his prayers, whole village of characters in a bangle, the forgotten dream perhaps, those faces forever eating their God! Mongol whose strange laugh can be heard most of the day; one in wheel-chair from just inside her half-door always waves and tries in vain to keep the hens out with walking stick. Peeping heads — row upon row of them like carved potatoes. Riding a pig to Dublin dressed in finest green; the man with wooden feet contemplating the great unknown — will never do him any good . . . Doodle a lost soul, can faintly hear —

'O would you like to swing on a star,
Carry moonbeams home in a jar,
Or would you rather be a pig . . .'

Something at the back, cat probably . . . Brennan doing cartwheels, standing on his head . . .

Morning is the funeral, coffin carried by four young men, some of the women weeping, they follow to the graveyard, it is lowered and priest shovels the first soil, lips his solemn words. See everything from work bench, village kind of fantasy world unto itself without knowing, the uneventful lives and routine. Dogs as well, Brennan's Bruno always goes stiff and howls when Angelus is rung; wee shaggy the piddler wherever he goes, the one eyed collie from Doyle's pub who fetches the

65

*Press.* Girl almost hysterical is led away, and later buying nails from Brennan says 'Wasn't that terrible sad now and she only twenty-four?'

Only sexton remains filling the hole, beats soil tight with flat of shovel, stamps with foot the sods into place, then carries the old door to back of bell tower. Waves to as mounts bicycle and pedals off a swaying shape to Doyle's . . . a hundred light years away!

And that's her tucked in for eternity . . . is working opposite a graveyard the place to really be?

There is a grinning clergyman looking in, sees, dear God what does he want? Father always hides in his bedroom, but he's knocking at the door now, will have to let him in.

'We've heard all about you.' Sort of mischievous look, holds out his hand and grips tightly for rather too long.

'So glad you've come to Kilkenny, not many of us left now you know! Will we see you at church on Sunday, could you come to lunch next week? The strawberries look very good and you'll meet some of the others.'

At table picks up a brooch.

'Fascinating, absolutely fascinating, a real artist I can see; you know I might just have a little job for you, we can talk about it next week.'

There's nothing like secrets!

He's a kind of bluff buffoon, looking across at the chapel says 'You're really amongst them here; but you know, they're honest and well behaved, couldn't wish for nicer neighbours really.'

Goes on a while . . . was up in Donegal for five years and knew uncle William well. Could even begin to half admire him in a sort of way, ministering to dwindling flock, faithful few every Sunday, perhaps church half full at Christmas and Easter, compared to the chapel packed!

Slaps pockets and from outside top brings a well worn watch with one strap missing. 'My heavens I must be off, have a meeting with the Dean, we'll be seeing you then.'

Strides across to his grey Morris Minor, which at first doesn't start, then stalls and powerless glides away silently . . . pushed by angels surely! Might be a good idea to go to church this Sunday, perhaps meet a few potential customers, . . . don't know a soul, and there's a dance in Kilkenny this Friday.

Park beside the castle's enormous classical entrance gate near tinkers on the Parade. High enough to take a double decker bus, what forgotten world's behind those walls?

Say these dances don't really get started until about ten or eleven, far too early, will dander down the main street. A butcher's shop displays pigs' heads and feet, large bowl of hearts and livers. Two tinker women begging from shop to shop, their little ones following with outstretched hands could make you weep, what century tread the dead of an obscene past? A crone who can't have washed for years passes with a basket of bones — are they for soup or dogs? Monstrous fat boy in greasy coat shuffles along shouting evening papers. Eyes a locked soul in the hideous folds. Lovely girl in a yellow sports car watching, O Lord there's something from a different age still lingering here. Narrow alleys lead off to dark places . . . a witch who can tell your future and cure the pox, brothel of Bridgets and Marys whose flesh is white as snow. Bells start to ring, priests appear, a Franciscan monk . . . indeed! Those books in the old home as a child used to read — were once bloody arm of the Inquisition! Will the strange primordial fear never leave? The light is low but still burns, in dreams, odd moments of realization, the words . . . words of Latimer to Ridley.

'Be of good comfort, Master Ridley. Play the man: We shall this day light such a candle, by God's grace, in England, as I trust shall never be put out.'

Book of Common Prayer and Glorious Revolution. Order

and reason and hard work and thrift . . . that superstitious lot
to flight! Ah no, didn't have to come, yet; climbing worn steps,
carved figures in walls and out to St Canice's, the sun has set.
Light a grey-blue, nothing is distinct but Round Tower and
shape of Cathedral, dark and mysterious inside, sit and . . .
it is all so familiar, rich colours of the altar glow, tombs of
soldiers and bishops on all sides . . .

Town is now lit, down kind of ladder steps to what must
have been a cellar, walls painted indigo with tanks of goldfish
set into. A juke-box blares *The Yellow Rose of Texas*, have to
shout to be heard, totally unreal through thick cigarette
smoke, men and women in groups at tables and bar counter,
fall partly silent when enter, with difficulty order half pint. In
the middle of them now, nice one in corner though, barmaid
not bad either . . . sounds like upper English accent beside.
About middle forties, nose verging plum, mocking eyes, thick
black hair beginning to grey, comfortable paunch, looks
rightly depraved.

'You wouldn't be the silversmith would you?' He says.
Without time to reply.

'What on earth brought you to this bloody place? They're
savages the lot of them, just look at that fine specimen of
Irish male over there.'

Obviously very drunk attempts to stand, raises his spilling
tankard and shouts 'To the fightin' men o' Cork!'

Some cheer loudly.

'What are you drinking?' And orders three pints, one for
his Bunter faced friend. Name is Dave Hitchcock, works for the
Kilkenny Gas works.

'He's a gas man you know!' Interrupts Bunter winking and
bursts out laughing at his own joke.

Hitchcock looks pained and empties his pint, wipes mouth
dry with back of hand, slides off high stool, 'Let's see what we
can find at this dance, Carlton isn't it?' To Bunter.

Main street together then, turn off a lane leads to music

getting louder . . . wonder what brought him to Kilkenny? Doesn't seem to quite fit, especially with that accent, working for the Kilkenny Gas works. Read only last week was losing money and leaks. Hardly the age to be going to dances looking for women . . . be a misfit at home suppose, someone here!

Lurid glow from side entrance, music pounding now, boys together stand about. Visit men's first — someone's been sick, whole place stinks something awful, the corrupted insides! Stand and all pee, fag ends float and God did really want to come to this? Hitchcock straightens his gaudy tie and combs hair to the dirty cracked mirror.

'Jes' will yo' look at the big pouf!' Says Bunter.

'At least I know how to handle women Mr Dunne, you can't even dance, you'll be back in your cold bed soon enough with nothing soft to keep you warm!' Leads on to the crowded dance floor bold as a rooster.

Can hardly move so packed, the sweating bodies press tight, Hitchcock eyeing the talent a few moments pushes way to one large girl and soon is lost. On stage four in blazing sequin tunics gyrate to words inaudible, the girls are wild eyed, some screaming hoarse watching them play, like that time in Dublin only wilder what madness to-night, are liberated, set free, holy men flee and prayers and promises forgotten now the Celtic mother takes each to highest point, taste that lost ecstasy . . . she looks perfectly wanton that luminous-like eye shadow, short skirt and jumper fit to burst, goes Hitchcock with another — laughing silly, and standing beside looks up and think yes, why not, yes, squeezed together . . . and gradually hold tighter around the floor.

O Ireland.

Why, what brought to this madness?

Her hair is freshly washed, kind of dark chestnut, glimpse raining outside, bit of punch up, drunken shouts, suspenders, Hitchcock has the scarlet woman on his knee!

Her name is Cathleen from Castlecomer.

Feeling faint, be the beer on an empty stomach . . . swirling faces, face could murder, crouched in the bog forever waiting with sharpened bronze, who shot a constable in the back at point blank range and ran all the way to confession where a sweating priest forgave him! These wildest imaginings . . . screaming in terror as Cromwell's Ironsides cut down, bowels spilling like rope to his young wife was raped twelve times and infant who saw never spoke again, all Ireland's anarchy here now, nothing changes ever . . . everyone stops to hear him sing the last *Kiss Me Quick* to a roar of delight, bows and stumbles exhausted behind curtain.

The silence deflates, breaks up, she slips away to cluster of girls queueing for coats, can see Hitchcock at the back wiping sweat from his forehead with a big spotted handkerchief, fizzy orange in one hand.

'Fancy a bite of supper then? There's nothing here.'

It is cold outside, streets glistening wet, cars starting up, couples against walls and entrances as one. Air of cooking food, Hitchcock rubs hands and says 'It smells good'.

And an open door, inside's a sort of kitchen, behind counter one armed man stirs huge tank of boiling chips, another holds what looks like pig's trotters. Again what age does one step into? Place of iniquity, castle cook house of some petty King O'Malley, lost that limb stealing cattle, was lucky to get back alive. Few dark travellers wait for left-overs. Wicked looking knife that, amazing how he can use one arm with such effect, works twice the speed netting chips and spooning the pinky white shapes on to stacked pages of newspaper, deftly wrapped is a mysterious bundle absorbing grease . . . parcel of papish fingers to chew on!

He orders two lots, will never eat it, maybe manage a chip or two, to his place on The Parade. Outside seems a fine four storey Georgian, looks very grand, but hallway's crammed with planks, ladder, cement bags, cans of this and that. Bits of toys trail up stairs, half eaten piece of bread . . . searches for

70

key and puts to Yale hole creakingly opens to huge room and slumped in low bursting armchair. Dunne dozing, grumpily complains, 'Will you put the bloody draught stopper back!'

'Don't mind him.' Says Hitchcock, 'Have a seat, I'll make coffee.'

An elegant room once, still gracious Adam style fire-place, stucco walls and ceiling falling away, big deep set wood panelled windows at each end, linoleum and thread bare carpet on the floor. Two black iron beds unmade, ugly varnished furniture, socks and honey stained underpants on line, odour of Old Spice, sour something and cigarettes. Paper bags burst with tins, soggy at the bottoms, ash trays full — Everybody is drinking Smithwick's Ale. One corner acts as sort of kitchen, piled with dirty dishes, he clatters about lighting gas ring and puts on aluminium kettle, rinses out enamel mugs and has just about enough milk.

'Do you have to make so much noise?' Complains Dunne.

Drops a plate on purpose and 'What did you say Mr Dunne?'

'I said you're an English bastard, a degenerate mother fucker if ever there was one!' Unwraps one of the packets and starts to nibble chips.

'You're not having any of those mate, you bloody sponger, owe me for last week's rent too!'

Snatches them away, and settles into the striped deck chair, packet on his lap and hungrily starts into. Kettle boils, gets up bringing supper, makes coffee that tastes foul, they argue back and forth, like pair of fighting cocks; would wonder why they live together at all. And opening the warm mess feel slightly sick.

'Well aren't you going to eat it then?' Says Hitchcock. 'Don't like to see good food going to waste, give it here.'

God help his guts . . . Dunne half undresses and gets into bed, then out again for an overcoat which he covers with. Hitchcock rambles on, half asleep, is asleep . . . as if from his dreams, 'Don't forget to turn the light out will you.'

71

Will have to be going, too far back to Mooney, odd pair, isn't Dunne something in the Ulster Bank, remember seeing him there surely . . . the door slowly opens and a little girl about four years old shyly peeps in, wearing a pale blue night-gown, bare feet, fair as the Sacred Heart picture. Slowly walks up to, smiles and says 'Hello'.

Where on earth did she come from? Must be family upstairs.

'Mummy and daddy were fighting you know.' Clambers up on Hitchcock's knee, snuggles into and 'I'm going to sleep with him now' and soon is lost. Strange house full, put a few lumps of coal on the dying fire, keep them warm, tartan rug around her, turn the light out and quietly leave.

Clock strikes three, sky clear and the moon is colour of quince above castle . . . and think of King Richard II who came to Ireland and lost his throne!

Enormous Garda passes, 'Isn't it a lovely night?'

Footsteps fade away into the silent and deserted city.

On the way back to Mooney the empty castles and towers float on thick blankets of mist.


Boil Brennan's brownest eggs, make toast and tea, then dress in only suit and when they're all inside at Mass slip away to protestant church. Lies much alone, could almost miss it low behind screen of yew trees. Just in time, last in, kneel at the back and through fingers count fifteen and six of a choir. Reverend briefly acknowledges and in a loud voice reads.

'If we say we have no sin, we deceive ourselves, and the truth is not in us; but, if we confess our sins, he is faithful and just to forgive us our sins, and to cleanse us from all unrighteousness.'

Then 'Let us humbly confess our sins unto Almighty God.'

Everyone kneels and with him say the Confession.

'Almighty and most merciful Father; We have erred, and strayed from Thy ways like lost sheep. We have followed too much the devices and desires of our own hearts. We have offended against Thy holy laws . . .'

Responses come automatic, just about know the whole service by heart, there are well polished brass plates on the pale walls to men killed in Boer and both World Wars. Few curious glance behind, not a pretty girl amongst them, dressed in thick things tweedy; young well scrubbed and sensible, couple like retired army types. Proud old bird in black, real emeralds on her knotted fingers, fair size, be worth a bit.

'O Lord, open thou our lips.'

'And our mouth shall shew forth thy praise.'

'O God, make speed to save us.'

'O Lord, make haste to help us.'

All standing.

'Glory be to the Father, and to the Son and to the Holy Ghost.'

'As it was in the beginning, is now and ever shall be; world without end. Amen.'

'Praise ye the Lord.'

'The Lord's Name be praised.'

Thumbing through . . .

. . . the Original Preface of 1549 concerning the evils of Romish Doctrine. Articles of Religion agreed upon by the Archbishops and Bishops for the avoiding of the diversities of opinions, and for the establishing of consent touching True Religion.

Psalm 95 is sung . . . and know are no longer really participating, only a viewer to this ceremony, the loveliest thing ever devised surely! Yet the Known brings a sort of comfort . . . some little hope amidst the darkness.

The first lesson is read . . . and service progresses, sermon that is absurd but nobody's listening, wonder what he'll have for dinner on Wednesday, his final words.

'The grace of our Lord Jesus Christ, and the love of God, and the fellowship of the Holy Ghost, be with us all evermore.'

'Amen.'

At the door he waits, shakes hands and chats with departing congregation, introduces some, say they will call, seem if anything amused at thoughts of a silversmith in Mooney. Captain Musgrave has a brass peacock plate got in India would like to bring along, needs polishing and few dents removed.

'Could you set an uncut amethyst in a silver ring for me?' Says a tall girl with prominent teeth.

'Where do you get your silver from?' Asks another wrapped in foxes.

Drive away in dull coloured Rovers, Morris Oxfords and Minors; the graveyard is rather overgrown, needs the scythe too . . . pull away tight grass from stone a rude carved IHS, lettering gone the fleeing woodlouse, tiny red spider is symbolic of Satan. Curious shaped cross by the hedge, Masonic device and crow. Died the year of Waterloo that one . . . bullock stares at chewing cud, bees on cornflower. Goes the Reverend, closing door and locking, doesn't see crouched behind stones, bolts the little iron gate and follows rest of congregation. Be happening all over the twenty-six counties now, the last Southern protestants are driving home to Sunday dinner. Word or two about the sermon, English papers from the village shop, then perhaps a sherry. Don't bother saying Grace, feeling full snooze in front of log fire, tea and cake, good film on television . . . they go to bed, but will they dream, dream of their protestant God and religion? That preaches He made the blind see, dead walk, turned water into wine, ascended into heaven and sitteth on the right hand of God the Father Almighty from thence he shall come to judge . . . all men.

Mooney is deserted, usual after Mass mess, change and . . . what? Sketch another brooch . . . the last protestant! Some fields away there's a game of hurling, tiny blue and yellow players chasing a ball with club shaped sticks.

Stamp finished pieces with maker's mark, weigh and count

five pendants, eight brooches, twelve rings, six bracelets and three bangles. Box, wrap in brown paper, tie with string and melt wax — drips thick on to the knots. Address to Assay Office, Lower Castle Yard, Dublin Castle.

Pouring rain run down to Post Office, whiffs unwashed nappies and boiled fish. Wait, wait for hours sometimes . . . hooded someone bowed to 'phone behind glass, grubby voting list, round Will's Woodbine reflects Gerty's face from back the sort of partition, is she asleep or made of alabaster? Supposed to be deaf, cough loudly . . . peers round.

'The silversmith eh!'

Takes parcel and puts on brass scales.

'Registered?'

Calculates on back of telephone book.

'Be three and six.'

Tears stamp and registration slip, laboriously makes out receipt — almost illegible the fallen letters. Drenched woman hurries in with packet for someone, Boston, Massachusetts.

Maggie Anne passing wrings hands and says 'Isn't it a shockin' day.'

Couple late for school again seem waterproof.

Priest's car by chapel, coming out can't avoid now comes over to.

'How are ye now? I meant to call, isn't it something to have a silversmith in Mooney!'

Shakes hands and surely this is the first time have ever spoken to a priest, let alone touch . . . was it like damp bread?

'I've been told you make some beautiful things . . .'

Short stooped and creamy bald head with darting eyes like trapped insects, hasn't shaved this morning, lips are thin lines of nicotine, contrast against false white teeth, suit frayed at cuffs, stains on shirt. Keeps talking and . . . the cold mad Northern voices rise and call.

'He's the Pope's disciple.'

'Product of a Church that's gross and corrupt.'

'Actually sold forgiveness once to pay for their high living.'
'Idolater.'
'Preach to their flock to outbreed protestants.'
'Know one haggard woman with a family of sixteen.'
'Drinker of Christ's blood.'
'Collector of sins.'
'Behind thick curtains in little varnished boxes.'
'First to burn their fellow Christians at the stake.'
Can see Titian's flame coloured Paul III . . .

Yet wasn't he friendly enough? Ordinary chap about his day, or was there an ignorance about those eyes . . . like the Reverend's are mad?

Bell rings and Tommy Walsh the sexton wants to know would there be a job for his son.

'He's just sixteen and a good steady lad, would be most willing to learn.'

Stands sheepishly by his father, nearly twice as tall, smile slowly spreading.

'Very quick with his hands, did well at Art and Woodwork when at the Kilkenny Tech you know.'

Both are soaked, son with no cap, look miserable.

'Says he'll go to England as there's nothing here to stay for, will break his mother's heart.'

Invite in, explain and offer tea which they refuse, leave and dander over to Brennan's, probably his idea should ask. Couldn't possibly afford it, hold the work up. And it rains all day and long into the night, can hear it on the roof, wind whistles a strange note . . . unhappy and despairing, weeping for all of them!

Tuesday is a wedding, work and watch them arrive, go into the chapel . . . emerge man and wife. Bride at least thirty, groom be in his forties, very dangerous that they say . . . pose for photographs, beaming together, then with best man and two bridesmaids in lime, wasn't one of them at the dance in Kilkenny? Lots of confetti and laughter, people really enjoying themselves, horns blaring to reception at the Metropole in Kilkenny.

And all the while Tommy's digging a grave!

Afternoon priest and few collect, man lifts linen covered box from back seat of car, must be baby they're going to bury. Takes under arm to graveyard, heads bowed, faintly his prayers carry . . . they quickly depart. Sky covers and wind picks up again blowing confetti away . . . without sin wouldn't the child go straight to heaven?

> Jesus loves me: he who died
> Heaven's gate to open wide;
> He will wash away my sin,
> Let his little child come in.

> Jesus loves me: he will stay
> Close beside me all the way,
> Then his little child will take
> Up to heaven, for his dear sake.

Fiddler playing at Doyle's . . . incomprehensible singing outside, Tommy drunk likely!

The rectory is square grey, up a drive under big gloomy trees. Wife Margaret has a glass eye and looks far too young for him. There are strawberries under nets in walled garden at the back, donkey grazing the front lawn, mangy spaniel dog and no children.

In drawing room before just lit fire, fearing something boiled over Margaret excuses herself to the kitchen. Reverend offers a drink and tells about the job he wants done . . . a silver communion box with cross of St Patrick somehow on the lid, for a Mrs Haughton in memory of her late husband. Sunshine streams through the high Georgian windows, highlights things silver well used and cared for, large oil painting in gilded frame of man in red uniform — stares at all the time. A pre-war

Wolseley draws up outside and two middle sixtyish ladies get out, excuses himself and goes to meet them.

Sherry makes giddy . . . hardly belong to this lot, really absurd . . . returning introduces a Lady Tollemond and Miss Spratt.

Don't have to say a word, just look interested and nod attentively. Complain about the weather and difficulty of getting help. Last one in the family way had to leave for Roscrea!

'They just haven't a clue when it comes to that kind of thing, the poor silly girls.' Says Lady Tollemond.

'And of course their religion doesn't help either!' Agrees Miss Spratt pushing away dog sniffing between her knees.

Margaret comes in again and sits on the sofa arm, has nice legs, smartly dressed and with glass eye a strangely attractive woman.

'My dear you're looking absolutely marvellous. Did Seamus McGrath do the garden for you yet?' Asks Lady Tollemond . . .

Grace is said, dinner's very good but not enough of it. Georgian silver spoons, forks, condiment and two fine Corinthian candlesticks. Ask can tell the dates, look about the seventeen nineties and Dublin hallmark. Engraved arms of Argent, a chevron between three crosses — flory ermine, came to him through paternal side.

'How much would they be worth?' Enquires Margaret.

'Really Margaret, are you thinking of selling them then?' He interrupts rather annoyed. She shrugs it off and fetches a big bowl of strawberries and jug of cream.

'Oh don't they look gorgeous.' Coos Miss Spratt. Everyone helps themselves.

Coffee is served back in the drawing room, can see sheep on the front lawn. Rush out and try to chase back . . only makes things worse, scatter all over the garden now, donkey braying wildly. He's like a crow that can't fly, arms uplifted, running this way and that . . . and Margaret's high laughter from the open window, head thrown back breasts pushed forward and long honey hair in disarray, ladies looking most worried behind her. He's puffing and turning deeper, mouth shut very tight.

Finally manages to get them back to the field, go inside, he doesn't say much, Margaret looking prettier now cheeks flushed. Pours more coffee, faint giggle still . . . and it is time to leave.

She'll be in for it!

Think of her all afternoon, as start communion box. Score four deep lines on square of silver sheet, cut away corners, bend up sides and solder. Simple lift off lid without hinge heavily textured, cross of St Patrick polished on an oxidised background.

Design her a golden rose will never make . . .

Postman like Solomon Eagle returns the parcel from Assay Office hallmarked. Set stones, lay marks, file, emery and polish each piece. By weekend collection is finished. Definitely different, couldn't have made the likes in London; like miniatures really, tiny worlds away — the way it is from window on Mooney. Last night Maggie Anne jumped over the chapel, priest chased the devil and Tommy saw God!

But will it sell? Have to go to Dublin early Tuesday morning and see.

Village still sleeping, sanctuary light a red glow, creamy sky spreads the first of new day. Black cat crosses leaving, be luck that . . . into New Ross and head for Enniscorthy the world is waiting, a few souls about now, stop for cows to milking, he raises his stick.

'A fine mornin' Sur.'

But does he see it?

His great Lord and Master crowned resplendent at every turn, whispering in the hawthorns, rippling up the Slaney, Robins about Ferns Castle, hush about the blue blue Blackstairs. On the road to Dublin this day wears the finest clothes.

Case of jewellery right, price list seems reasonable enough, pity have to sell them in a way . . . crossing through Stephen's Green . . . with her head so high and ankle just right across to Dawson Street, will never see again. There's a little death with each pretty face! Down Grafton Street, Wicklow and soon the Castle to leave communion box in for assay. Little brick building on its own; ring and slide at counter opens to strange youth takes and shuts like lightning back again. And soon behind locked doors they'll strike Hibernia, crowned harp and square V. In hallways can see wooden chairs with crowns carved on. First RIC murdered there that Easter weekend who would remember him now? A bullet through his heart for Ireland!

Worst part of it now, into shop most grand, and taken up stairs by buyer to small room overlooking Grafton Street. Spread each piece on blue velvet, asks for price list very business like and compares, a minute is eternity . . . asks meaning of this and that, excuses and 'phones for another . . . enters dark suited, vivid mustard tie and pearl pinned nods and appraises table. Both go out, are two shadows behind frosted glass, return and say smiling 'We'll take the lot.'

Bewley's with coffee calculate came to nearly one hundred and fifty pounds, promise of more orders if moves well, another cup and currant bun. She spoons three heaped of brown sugar, and sips it, too hot, no doubt aware that all the world is at her feet, nails painted peach and the long delicate fingers clasp . . . all Dublin!

Buy a hat in R Tyson.

Browse through books and all things Switzers and Brown Thomas.

Brass plate The French Huguenot Fund!

In the Shelbourne Grill order fat omelette and chips, the protestant Bishop of Cashel two places down contemplates menu. It is very warm and the well dressed well fed people's natter makes a pleasant monotone, nothing matters now, secure and safe this lunch hour. Fall asleep on deep old leather upstairs an ornate lobby papered Cardinal Red, butters and creams, prints of eighteenth century Dublin . . . on their note-paper draw a benevolent deity . . . waiters come and go.

Everyone is rich and happy in Dublin today!

They've elected a new Pope and papal flags are flying everywhere.

It is a shame to have to go; will drive to Kilkenny, have a good supper and drink at the Hotel, maybe see Hitchcock there — is most nights.

Drinking all alone in corner greets hushed 'Did you see the new barmaid over there?'

Behind the pink marble topped counter bent at something in blue smock and raven hair tied in bun. Looks up, eyes meet and . . . O Jesus! She's the best looking girl ever saw yet, could ever. Hardly be seventeen, real green eyes set the shield shaped face on long white neck, and ordering two pints smiles perfect teeth, the soft Kilkenny accent.

'There we are now.'

'Bit of all right what?' Enthuses Hitchcock rubbing hands, 'Asked her to the dance tonight, only laughed in me face the saucy scrubber. Have a go yourself.'

He's right, will never see the likes again, before place gets too crowded.

'Well maybe I will and maybe I won't, don't get off work until ten this evening, a little after at the front perhaps and only perhaps.' And continues her job — making tea bags.

Cold waiting in the car and long past ten . . . will she ever come? Down the steps suddenly gracious as a queen in short white coat and hair now down to her waist, opens the passenger side door and gets in beside.

'I've been looking at you from the highest window for this last twenty minutes trying to make up my mind.' Starts to laugh, moonshine and diamond dust . . .

'Dance be nearly over now, let's go for a short drive, will have to be back by twelve, the doors are locked then.'

Anywhere . . . down a narrow lane by ruined mill park, overlooks the rushing Nore, tumbled boulders and rocks, moon bright above, catches her face shining excitement and kiss and kiss and kiss . . . a sudden torch light and deep voice.

'Are ye all right now?'

Is a beaming Garda at the window.

'Sorry to be disturbin' ye, I wasn't sure anyone was there.'

Leans elbow on the roof.

'Aren't ye the silversmith from Mooney? Is it rings and things like that you make, where would one learn that kind of work now?'

She tries hard not to laugh as he goes on and on . . . and finally 'I'll be leavin' ye now, goodnight.'

Laugh and laugh together, tears down her cheek, taste salt.

'I never thought the big eejit would ever leave, are you really a silversmith?'

A large landrace sow is running up and down ears flapping squealing on the opposite bank with litter after. Strange sight in the eerie light, deep blues and greens, waters sound and this Eileen Cumiskey, warm and soft and lovely and could only be for all time . . .

'You'll have to take me back now.' Says.

The gaunt grumpy doorman looks disapproving as she hurries up the steps just in time, and the door is locked . . . and from her tiny window at the very top of the old hotel she waves and waves, her long raven hair tumbling down, blows a final kiss and gone.

Can hardly work thinking of her. Eileen, Eileen Cumiskey, catholic no doubt with a name like that. Why a girl like that wasting herself working as a barmaid? Lively, intelligent, quick as a hawk, doesn't seem to fit at all, where does she live apart from the hotel? Do anything to be with her again tonight.

Start a bangle with words deeply engraved — 'Wealth shall

he offer who longs for a maiden's love.'

Someone has draped a gravestone with the rosary.

Evening brings Hitchcock and Dunne want to go fishing at Inistioge, him eager to find out about Eileen.

'How'd you make out then; is she from Kilkenny? Never seen her before, only been at the hotel for a few days.'

'Don't tell him anything, the big randy pervert, Jes' at your age too!' Interrupts Dunne.

So go in gas works van to Inistioge . . . without any luck, never really much good with the fly, catches in weeds, reeds; Hitchcock taking wrong step, brings water over his boots.

'O shit!'

Fills the valley so quiet. Go and drink in the Spotted Dog, dries his socks before the fire, two great ugly feet and hairy legs . . . this time tomorrow will be with Eileen . . . they're both knocking it back, can't keep up with them. Outside it's quite dark, the days are getting shorter. Leaving Hitchcock warns, 'Watch it my man, she's only a scrubber in spite of her looks!'

But he's drunk.

And half way back to Mooney he stops for a leak, sounds a great gush of relief into a puddle, must have peed a fortune over the years. Dunne's got hiccups for goodness sakes . . . and all under the vast incomprehensible heavens, milky way, bursting stars and new born suns, aeons of immeasurable time her image dancing . . . completely unaware he shakes his big limp dick dry, bends a leg and fastens fly. Dunne a mighty yawn.

Just a little down from the hotel then, be late again suppose, aren't they all like that, probably won't even turn up, is a cold thought . . . become talk of the place soon, the silversmith and new barmaid, but who gives a damn! Be plenty of time for a good long drive this evening looking at the map, never been to Cashel. Bang bang on the side and she's smiling at, looks stunning.

'Well! Where are you going to take me this evening?'

And leaving the city she holds hand tightly, now take all
Ireland's heart beating true and fair, the years were spent for
just to know her? Must have been, what else compares . . .
the other Irish hardly know.

'I know this road well, Paddy takes me who drives the turf
lorry.' Says thoughtfully.

Wonder, but dare not ask who Paddy is, through Ballyline
into Tipperary a different world of sombre green and breath-
less plained where pale mountains call.

'Cashel, Cashel of the Kings.' Muses, and for a moment
seems far away.

Know names of all the mountains in sight, Comeragh,
Monavullagh, Knockmealdown and Galty sound music from
her lips. And quite suddenly the great Rock of Cashel, stark
and bold, high against the evening sky, a string of starlings
above its jagged old towers and gables.

'Is neambh e.'

Mischievous look when ask the meaning.

'Means it's heaven, what they tell us the English took away!
You must have been there. I'm going next year.'

Will follow if needs be . . . interesting that Irish, odd sentence, word from a dead tongue, probably knows the Fenian
Proclamation by heart, taught at school! Yet her being so
gives feelings added strength, could embrace her whole wild
race, clan Cumiskey spell cast and doomed these parts brawling
and treacherous with much prayer and songs to music that is
mad. Hand in her hand never leaves enter the strange place
through archway . . . and the ruins reel on shifting green, unreasonable shape stands like a deformed prophet surrounded
by the living dead, walls.

'I saw a new heaven and a new earth, for the old heaven and
old earth had passed away.'

It is the last day . . . nearly over now gazing down from roof-
tops the great fertile wheel of Tipperary, river winds, willows
and bones of a friary.

Sit together until it is almost dark.

And looking back on road to Clonmel, it is floodlit, floats in a soft pool of darkness.

Through forests of silver fir and spruce so silent, scent the air, past shrine to Virgin, shells rounded sea stones set in cement and wild flowers at her feet in jam jars. Snuggles close, hair almost touches the floor, fingers through, like fine thread. Downwards a whole expanse of country in the last light. Clonmel is undisturbed and unaware this momentous day — was like any other; some stand at corners, pubs and melancholy eyes follow through, for them there's nowhere to go and nothing to do.

Buy bars of nut chocolate and two fat yellow pears at late closing shop in Dungarvan. Everything is so real as she wraps them in a white paper bag, adds up and hands to, two shillings and fourpence. Rows of cheap fizzy drinks, galvanized buckets and bristly brush heads behind, and all the while knowing she's waiting.

Silence that needs no interrupting, will never get her back by midnight now, but she doesn't seem to care.

'Was only for a few pounds before the New Year.'

Sea breeze now and glimpse white breakers on a long biscuit coloured shore.

At Dunmore East the harbour is crowded with fishing boats, electric lights on masts cast slow rocking shadows. Few scattered dead fish on pier and decks look like bars of silver from the deep. The amber woods and bright painted sides, numbers, one called Molly Malone. Thick sweatered men bend about nets and boxes, cigarettes glow, sea is calm, sea that will take her to England . . . no!

Eat the chocolate, juice from pears falls on to, gives a tiny handkerchief that smells of lavender. Keep. The warm cab is a cell of security . . . against world that cannot be kept out for long. And asking the time her mood abruptly changes.

'I'll really lose the job now, all be in bed, Mam will be so upset!'

Starts to cry when suggest to take to her home instead. Would she come back to Mooney and stay the night?

Hesitates, and 'Well, yes; we'd better go now.'

Hope they're all asleep in Mooney . . . seem so as both go in. Will put the kettle on and make some coffee.

Asks 'Whatever brought you here?'

And to herself ' 'Tis what I'm trying to escape from.'

Can have bed, borrow pyjamas too too large.

'You can come in now.' Laughs when bring up the long mirror.

'Don't I look a right fool?'

And 'You'd better go now.'

In the next room can't sleep in the chair most awkward, go down to workshop and start her a brooch, pick two tiny blue agates be nice; the night is breaking . . . and Eileen never heard is looking at.

'You can sleep with me if you like!'

Gone ten and still asleep, her face is upturned to the skylight, trace firm jaw line and nose a faint hump in middle, tiny ears and hands . . . who is she? Not much to eat, go down to Brennan's.

'Was it you that came in so late last night?' Enquires searching for the last sliced pan, his great bottom to, 'Sounded very like your bus now!'

And wonder who else heard or even saw! Pour tea and make her toast, put on the tin Guinness tray and take to. She is awake, head resting on forearm and reading *The Pilgrim's Progress.*

Looks up, 'Isn't this very grand, breakfast in bed from the silversmith of Mooney.' Eats three slices and sips tea, better stay inside until it's dark say; village be in a buzz otherwise.

'Ah sure don't I know, I'll make your dinner if you like.'

Her stockings, filmy slip, bra and things are draped over chair, on her blouse is a pioneer pin! See Maggie Anne coming out of the chapel looks up, couldn't possibly see in, if she keeps to the back and draws curtains more, should be all right. Nice enough day, better do some work, reassures 'I'll be fine, come down to see you in a while.'

Change the blue agates to same size cornelian and aventurine, are two oval bodies that hold each other; it goes very slow, the footsteps directly above. Don't know what to do, upsets everything . . . Coming downstairs radiant and fresh, hair brushed gleaming and just a touch of make-up with mug of steaming coffee, 'I thought you would be likin' this, your kitchen's a right mess!' Goes over the room like a magpie.

'What's this for?'

'They're so pretty.'

'Is that a real emerald?'

'O Lord look at the little priest saying his prayers, you anti Christ!'

And picking up a tiny gold pin, 'Be the first time I've ever touched real gold, Mam has an old locket but it's only plated.'

The Angelus starts to ring, half crosses herself and catching look, 'I suppose you're a bold protestant?'

And then leaves the room, legs racing behind banisters and touch of slip. Was she joking or not? Wouldn't know what to make of that indeed . . .

Silence . . . sounds of activity from kitchen, noise of dishes and kettle boiling . . . something cooking . . . then 'You can come and get it now.'

Hardly recognise the place, cleaned dishes, pots and pan all neatly put away, table scrubbed with fluffy scrambled eggs and buttered bread to eat. 'It's the best I can do, your cupboard is bare, there's a dead mouse under the sink, wretched thing gave me an awful fright.'

Afternoon passes, watches work, finish early, bit of bacon and fresh bread from Brennan again. Always seems to taste better when someone else makes it. Takes fat from plate, 'Sure that's the best part of it.' Dry as she washes, hums a low tune — sad . . . Irish, folds the tea towel side of sink.

When the village street is empty drive right up to the front door, gets into the back quickly and moves up to a few miles on. Directs back to Kilkenny, on out and going through the village of Freshford turns to and says 'There's a ceili in Urlingford tonight.'

Very well then . . . won't have a clue though that kind of thing.

To an old green painted World War I army shed, music fit to lift the roof. Seems well known the nods and looks, sense she's annoyed with clumsy movements, and resting goes off with another. So natural together, the co-ordinated steps, can really dance, the swirling figure all eyes upon, certainly enjoying herself. Feel right out of place now.

A foreigner.

Sitting immobile to the music that brings tears, sounds of Ireland making a whirlpool of the brain. Disintegrates everything held and brings forth emotions never knew before.

Lord Inchiquin.

The Curragh

Haymakers' jig.

Returns to though thank God! Perspiring and right out of breath, 'Paddy's always good for a laugh.' Must be one that drives the turf lorry suppose!

All the boys are looking at her, the girls seem glad she's back with.

Towards Freshford same way came, turn up a narrow road and hill, at crossroads says 'You needn't go any further now, it's an awkward lane.'

Slow farewell and promise to meet tomorrow afternoon again, she finally slips off, can just see her white coat in the dark fading away . . . to where?

Thatched cabin of sixteen, father great bear of a man in the IRA. So what! It won't make any difference, not the way feel . . . does she exist at all?

Take out the tiny handkerchief that smells of lavender and

89

says so. In a way could understand why they keep relics! Everything is upside-down.

She wants to go to confession in Kilkenny! St Mary's Cathedral. Most emphatic . . . was it the other night — nothing happened or her conscience about going out with a protestant. Aren't things supposed to be different now after Pope John?

In love with her there's no doubt, take, whatever she wants can have . . . together going into the big almost white cathedral, sit towards the back; good few others, some pray, click of the rosary beads, take their turns to go into the confessionals . . . never feel right in a place like this, more a sort of temple than church. The grotesque statues and gruesome paintings of the fourteen stations, blood dripping from wounds and his flesh the colour of lard, really go in for the visual, all those little penny candles burning for the dead isn't it? Virgin up there of painted wood . . . and those varnished purple curtained boxes with priests behind. What sins she has to confess God only knows it's ridiculous . . . she's in for a long time.

If Finn or any saw now they'd think be better dead . . . and those dark voices warn again.

'The turncoat.'

'Sold his soul for a bit of tail.'

'You'll sign the children away.'

'Has he no backbone, a jellyfish.'

'Priests will never leave alone.'

'No birth control remember, who can afford more than two children these days?'

'Big families aren't decent.'

'Sure remember wee Harry Flynn and the priest around asking why they didn't have more children.'

'The cheek.'

'I'd have kicked him out.'

'But they have the fear of the devil in them, what can they do?'

'Expect you to give them a percentage of all earned.'

'Peter's Pence.'

'Sure the Pope's a billionaire. Owns the Holy Bank of Rome, or is it the Holy Ghost? Either one. Have huge financial investments the world over, and remember what Our Lord said about the rich man!'

'Wouldn't it make you sick.'

'Aren't they livin' in the lap of luxury, driving the big cars and best food in Dublin's finest hotels.'

'And old Willie who won five pounds on the bingo last week, the parish priest was round the next day for his cut, poor soul, what could he say?'

'Ignorance, just plain ignorance. Have a look about them don't you think?'

'Yes!'

'Look what they did when the Council built those lovely new houses for them in Downpatrick. Turned them into slums, real eyesores, and the children barefoot all over the place.'

'Should be made to clean up or get out, have no respect for property whatsoever.'

'Animals.'

'Imagine her teaching his children to say the rosary before bed . . .'

Sent to flight by her at last beaming now, out together and at the door she dips her fingers into a font of holy water and sprinkles all over.

'You horrible heretic.'

Teasing with the devil in her eyes, she starts to run, run after, laughing silly until catch and kiss and don't care who's looking at or not.

Ask what sins she's confessed.

'Ah now I wouldn't be telling you that.' Looks like an imp.

'It's not for the likes of you to know!'

Now that's an end to that.

Then 'Will we go to the pictures tonight, we'd be just in time?'

The film is called *Blue Hawaii* and is so bad it's good with colour and music and singing and she's happy enough watching it a face of delight turning to all the while . . . where will all this end, it's happening so quickly?

Later in the car 'I'll have to collect my things from the hotel, they said I'd have to go after being away all that night — aren't you terrible.'

In a rage now down the steps again with a small flimsy case tied with string, muttering to herself 'The old bitch, wouldn't give me the pay for the few days worked.'

And leave her back to that mysterious crossroads again, wont't let go any further.


Her religion doesn't matter, father certainly wouldn't care, could she? You'd never know, does she even feel the same way at all? So go and find out and court this Eileen Cumiskey. Never thought would be like this.


Buy pink and white carnations, Dairy Milk and Apple Blossom perfume. Sitting on the gate by crossroads and old Fertagh Round Tower some fields away, a green ribbon in her hair, skirt above knees very saucy, tiny bunch of rose-hips in one hand.

'Isn't it a beautiful day, are those really for me?'

'Carnations!'

Tears boxes open like a child, 'Such lovely chocolates, and this, what's this? Perfume!' Hugs and kisses . . . dabs a bit on neck and lets sniff.

'No one ever gave me presents like these.'

Drive the County Laois direction. Another and another ruined castle climb. Underneath an old bridge shelter from the rain, then blow dandelion seeds . . . is this really happening or in a dream?

Drawing the curious shaped crosses her chatter all the while.

'What did you make today?'

'Will you take me to Dublin next time?'

'There's a dance in Kilkenny on Friday.'

'Ah will you look at the little frog!'

At Jerpoint Abbey picks tiny wild flowers and makes a daisy chain.

Thinks the Long Cantwell looks very cross and makes a face at him.

On the Blackrock Mountain slaps for being so bold and tries to run away.

And then one day at Holycross 'Will you miss me when I go to England soon?'

'I won't let you go, I'll . . . marry you instead.'

'O'

She gazes across the slow moving Suir for seems an age.

'You're a protestant. But I don't care, yes I will, yes I will I will.'

Then 'Are you really sure?'

As sure as that heron stands sentinel in the reeds.

She gets up and walks on some, looking worried, plucks the high grass and turning to.

'The priest's after Mam for me going out with a protestant, threatened to pass at the communion rail if continue to see!'

Will shoot the dog if needs be! Go and see, put a stop to that nonsense, have to anyway now probably be married in his church there!

'Mam's very upset, but says it's up to me though.'

Then as if she doesn't want to say, 'She's not my real mother you know!' And very slowly as if opening an old wound starts to tell . . .

The rooms were large, ceilings high, cold, colours brown on brown, rows of iron cots and tiny faces through the bars. Would stare at each other for hours . . . those faces, faces behind bars.

Unknowing.

Was the order of things when life began in a cage with Jesus Christ crucified on every wall.

And the nuns in black, so black black black, black as death. Each carried a long leather strap at side to teach the little children the rule of things . . . and quickly learnt was different, bastard, illegitimate, child of sin, mistake, unwanted, mother's shame and father's wild oats sown.

Could hardly sleep for fear of wetting bed and wake to them. Dressed in coarse smocks and hob nailed boots — smallest hob nailed boots in the whole world! File down to breakfast at long scrubbed wooden tables. 'Bless us, O Lord, and these Thy gifts, which we are about to receive from Thy bounty, through Christ Our Lord. Amen.' Grabbed bread and tin mug of milk, arms around guard, protect from hungry neighbours.

Ring a ring a rosies in the big stone yard, catch the ball and their tiny voices for a while; wondered what'd behind the wall: to be like the birds that flew near the kitchen, could fly away, so far away . . . reach that heaven maybe, he looked so kind.

Most Sacred Heart of Jesus,
I place all my trust in Thee.

When clouds parted the way was pure blue . . . loved colours
. . . pretty silly things.

That strange woman might occasionally call, just sat and
always wept, face rough and raw, chain smoked, left something knitted, bag of aniseed balls, until told by nun must go.

There was crying everywhere and everyday.

Were seasons and few surprises, all ever knew the days to
weeks and years until nearly eight. And spring when the cherry
tree was mass of pink blossom, a new dress and shiny leather
shoes, parcel of things too. The ambulance called and took,
nun and few others waved away through gates, could see from
back a world that was dancing all things to the sky. Ordinary
people, houses, all sorts of animals the endless road through
villages and town with shops that sold everything. Driver
bought an ice-cream, didn't dare eat such a thing until he took
a bite and reassured. Tasted so sweet and creamy, like nothing
on earth and not a single one in sight.

Then to that crossroads. Door opened to a curious crowd
was waiting, watched. Children intent as woman stepped forward and said 'Call me Mam'. Took by the hand and led up
the narrow potted lane to cottage with all kinds of flowers
growing and goat tethered at the front.

Kitchen warm and cosy, upstairs showed tiny room and bed,
own chest of drawers, chair and faded photograph of Kevin
Barry with shamrocks around. Mam made tea with bread and
butter, as much jam as she could put on, face soon a sight, and
in the mirror began to laugh, first time had laughed like that
ever. Could do more or less what wanted, in the garden and
fields, just sit and take it all in. View towards Freshford, a
thick wooded rise, big house and shell of tower. Evenings by
the fire watched so many different faces flicker, fears, thoughts
. . . would the nuns take back, could stay forever? Put to bed
with hot water jar and paraffin lamp — no darkness now . . .
morning was good to know that yesterday was real.

Watched Mam milk the goat, collect eggs, brought out to

95

show Father Keane who stopped at gate in car. Appraised, eyes met for a second, bowed head. 'Isn't she very shy?' Said Mam.

'She'll be bold enough soon, now don't be too soft on her.' Warned, 'God Bless.' Lifted hand and drove away.

Brother and sister Brophy called, judged like newly purchased calf, 'Pretty some day all right, but she's too skinny, would thought you'd have picked one with a bit more meat.'

'She'll fill out well and good, keep me company and be handy about the house, with the money from the Council every month too.'

From top of the stairs playing thought she couldn't hear, let alone understand... that had no right to be here... anywhere!

Deegan children up the road told by parents not to play with, work of the devil! But met the way to school, brought sandwiches and tuppence a week for cocoa; in the one roomed building that had a big map of Ireland rolled down from the ceiling. Out at two, scattering the country ways was trickabouts, past Father Keane's big house, orchard of ripe apples and pears at side could almost reach . . . if it wasn't for that housekeeper shaking his fine white linen tablecloth from back door.

Home fetched water from the pump, gathered sticks to light the morning fire. Took goat to graze the verges. Walked all the way to village for half a stone of potatoes, pig's head and fat bacon for the poor on tick — can take or leave!

Could see up the drive where Major Maxwell lived, two ponies always grazed right in front of the big windowed house underneath chestnuts. The door opened and he descended steps all thick tweeds with dogs, daughters in black riding caps, jerseys and jodhpurs, tumbled into the shooting brake, crunched slowly to the gates, turned and didn't even notice half in the ditch with heavy bags, followed out of sight, looked at the lovely old house again . . and again, could just make out the carved desk, chairs and twisted lampstand from inside the warm depths.

It would be nice to be a protestant, but then some say they'll all go to hell!

Hopped over the stile to ancient stone cross in just cut corn fields, stands strange, stark keeper of secrets against the golden stubble and stooks, crows having a feast fly off, bold robbers strut about so black, black as the nuns were. Supposed to be holy ground, said a prayer, crossed . . . and the cold dead pig's head with human eyes and dried blood on snout stared lifeless from the paper bag, seemed to know the answer though, but couldn't tell. What's behind stars, end of space, why the sun always rises and moon shines at night, oceans and tides, vast rivers and continents, from birth to death the endless stream of light and consciousness that must end . . . to new dawn or total night? All in a pig's skull, in a field one summer day in the heart of Ireland!

No Lady's fingers thinned beets, turnips and mangolds for two bob a drill the land about Fertagh Round Tower; autumn picked potatoes. Most Saturdays put fresh flowers on the chapel altar, swept and polished, liked being there, another world, the coloured glass and rich things, always spoke in whispers.

Visits from the welfare lady most months, inspected clothes, hair and bed for lice. Woman who saw at the home on birth-days and first communion. But knew was mother now and hated, hid behind hedge without a tear until saw her leave.

Sent a chicken on the Limerick bus when had the measles once.

Feared Mam's son from Tipperary, bicycled over to stay some weekends. Late evenings always home drunk from the village like a mad thing. Wanted to touch and sit on knee when Mam was out, threw boiling water at with a vengeance once, he cursed and called 'You little bastard, be all's you're any good for anyway!' Leaned back of chair underneath door knob, half opened window, could squeeze through and on to galvanized lean-to case he tried again. Couldn't sleep then, they said he kicked his pregnant wife in the stomach, was an awful miscarriage!

Trip to Dublin the most exciting day of life. Zoo rode an elephant, trailed around the Dail and Dublin Castle, Master's voice became so emotional places, showed where men were shot for Ireland and their blood ran in torrents. Photographed at Independent House, free bag of sweets at Lemon's Pure Sweets Factory. The big boats at Dun Laoghaire waiting, would take away . . . one day.

Day the Kilkenny Hunt all reds and galloping horses straggled across the autumn landscape, ran outside for better view. Major's daughter Daphne reined up at cottage, slightly bending 'Could I have a glass of water please?' And Mam quick as never saw before fetched her best filled with lemonade was saving for Sunday. Gave a faint smile and 'Thank you indeed'. So high on the fine dapple horse now, all saddle and leather straps, parts metal glinted and jangled. Had to admit looked so very smart in the close fitting habit . . . picture persisted for such a long time.

For cottage was really mean, damp and cold, when it rained great patches appeared on the walls, nose always running, Mam's lungs began to wheeze, had to go out and spit the thick greeny slime, sometimes saw in the grass. And old Paddy Kennedy from God knows where for over a year now asleep in the next room. Gave Mam his money from the welfare each week; hands like a leper from rickets as a child, could only use two fingers for eating and lighting chalk pipe. Thumped on the partition with stick for pot to be emptied, head covered with blankets — an eye! And thought the old viper as poured out the back, wished he'd die! Had to mash his potatoes and cabbage with bit of fat meat, teeth that would eat you on the chair beside, couldn't avoid touching them to put the tray down. He even smoked in bed. Used to peep from the window to see relieving self behind laurel bushes, the pale bottom against green. Noticed once, raised arm and shook, 'Geeat away on thar!'

Remembered first kiss at a wake, Ellen Quinn lay in her coffin the front room, died from a blood clot having fifth child. Husband home from England for the wake, his mouth was full of cake and he didn't seem to care. Mam busy all morning for ten bob preparing the body — washed, plugged with cotton wool, sealed eyes with white of egg, closed mouth and put on a dark shroud. Arranged hands in praying position tied with Rosary beads. Made up altar on the dresser, lit two candles, placed crucifix and bowl of holy water. Alone for a while looked at the body so so at rest . . . in the white silky lined box . . . then Liam somebody or other came in very sudden himself upon . . . and luckily old Mrs Donovan came in, exclaimed 'In front of the dead, God save us!'

Glared at all evening, helping make pot after pot of tea, sandwiches, fruit cake, biscuits, pouring port wine and stout . . . the voices long into the night.

'God rest her soul.'

'May she be at peace.'

'And not yet thirty.'

'Maybe she's better off where she is, sure what was there here for her?'

But the music which uplifted, transferred elsewhere, with magic feet and rushing blood, soon the best for miles around. Learned at school and every dance and competition went, had dress of green and golden sash to wear, shamrocks and harps stitched: won cups and medals. All that really mattered — the dancing and music, echoed a call of long ago . . . the sounds that changed everything for a while . . . would go to England as soon as could.

. . . while Father Keane had his early tea of bacon, eggs, mushrooms and extra well done beef sausages, roll of freshly baked white bread — indulged in the crinkly crusts at both ends first. Could see on the road through apple trees munch munch, and thought she's grown in the right places without a doubt munch munch, bound to lead to trouble sooner or later, usually does munch munch, munch. A final cup of tea, knows shouldn't but had another slice of bread munch munch, be better off in a convent munch munch, could never be a nun though munch munch, born out of wedlock! Lit a cigarette and pondered the devil.

Fourteen and school at Kilkenny. Hitched rides and saved money claimed from welfare for bus fares. Had to be so careful though, things they'd try to do! Was nice to be in Kilkenny, made a change, the people, things to do and see. Friends with quite a few, invited back to their homes — always liked that. Looked forward to it every day, was never much else but the dances really, worked hard and passed every exam; so anxious to leave.

Near the end of last summer term interviewed by Brendan O'Ronan the bank manager for a summer job. July to September worked in the big bank house for forty-five shillings a week with meals was very good. Mrs O'Ronan was so nice, kind and considerate, treated like own daughter almost, eldest boy at Clongowes Wood, daughter in France with the Irish Consulate. But Brendan was something else indeed. Behind the grey suits and polished ways would try to get whenever the chance. Making the beds, putting linen in closet, across the kitchen table middle of baking tarts; even lured down to vault once, should have known better. Thought was a kind of right, fair game, good sport and used to show the naked natives from his *National Geographics.*

Would drive up to the cathedral every Sunday, him and the wife smart as you will; if they could only see him as saw that first day exposing it like child with new toy gun! But was far too quick for him, almost gave up in the end. Definitely worth it all though, the food, and nice things, week at Blackrock with whole family. Would never have had the heart to tell wife.

Then this year an English nurse came over and showed colour slides of the big hospital in London, would have own flat, interesting work, the best thing to do rather than stay in Kilkenny...

Looking at intently 'Do you still want to marry me now?'
Hold so tight yes yes, green and catholic and seed flung mystery, planted this mad sad country to nourish . . . all could ever hope for . . . she's Ireland, and much more.

This time will take her right home . . . the cottage is very small and stands out white-washed against the darkness. Tears away and runs to door — opens a stream of light, frames her figure dancing, a final wave, closes, and all the world is so empty and dead.

Order a diamond that's rather small but colour good, set alone in platinum on plain band of red gold — is a droplet of rare water, miraculous point of light reflecting the rainbow. Put in tiny satin purple box edged with silver. With the brooch she should be more than pleased.

Passage East the river gives way to sea and copper coloured cliffs, lighthouse, tower and village on the other side. Was it these parts they first came? Born of the fell fire-king, a spark-let prince to dart his bolt of icy fear in Erin's quaking heart! Pray for the curling mists to dissolve, keep from black and heavy armoured columns, advance and wheel their ghastly holy banners high . . . to a small cove with only life sea birds about. Scramble over sand and mustard lichen rocks, sit in the fitful sun and sea-spray touching, give Eileen the brooch and ring. The scene will be engraved for long as live.
Has the equinox been passed?
Is time running out?
Here on the very edge of Ireland with her, long hair a dark wind-swept cloud, cheeks touch of rose contrasting the eternal rocks and pounding sea, gulls wail, cormorant dives, mouth cold . . . clips the brooch on laughing, 'It'll amuse me forever, the poor little souls.' Then ring on fits perfectly, now like a ballerina kicks off shoes, from point to point dances . . The Faerie Queen, holds up this way and that, the finger of God

touches her hand sparkling. As if in a trance, from water to land to sky leaps and falls a dream, skirt whirling a fan, whole body possessed by spirits could never hope to know or understand...

Who was her father?

There's none like her from any around these parts, mother suppose but the father . . . she collapses beside. Lies on back, bosom heaving great gulps, closes eyes and as if reading own thoughts 'There'll never be another day like today for us.'

After a while rolls over, cups forehead in arms, 'Will you see Father Keane about it next week? Shouldn't be so much trouble now the old bishop is dead!'

Burst the bladder wrack walking back . . . and nearing Kilkenny, 'Let's go and see him before he's buried.'

'Who?'

'The bishop you silly goose.'

Lies very grand in St Mary's. The people file slowly past his ornate coffin in front of the altar. Looks as if waiting the call for his triumphant entry into heaven, dressed in rich woven golds, purple and purest white, gloved hands a very large ruby ring, crowned with mitre, lips uncannily red.

> Here I stand, on two little chips,
> Do come and kiss my ruby red lips.

Does God really care for his fat soul? And moving on she turns to, 'He gave very few dispensations you know!'

Sprinkles with holy water again laughing!

Says 'We'll make one of you yet!'


Or as they'd think an appointment with the devil himself! That time in Downpatrick with Auntie Annie in the butcher's shop, one was buying an awful lot of pork chops and thick T bone steaks. He had a stomach like a pregnant woman and a habit with buttons all down the front. His hair was greasy, his nose was hooked, and with all that dead flesh he was going to eat and the way he half smiled at and looked — would

103

probably eat too!

Just a little uneasy collecting Eileen for this meeting, she's a long time in coming, looking back again such a fright stands an old woman in a black shawl!

'She'll not be keepin' ye long now, come on up and sit by the fire.'

Must be Mam, 'The priest's been giving me a hard time, but don't be afraid of him, stand your ground, they're only mortals like rest of us.' As leads to cottage, stoop to small kitchen and Eileen combing her hair that's nearly dry in front of an open fire. Opposite could only be Paddy Kennedy bent double sucking pipe, half rises and 'Evenin' now'. There's holy pictures, souvenirs from Tramore and some photographs of Eileen at school — in floral smock, Fair Isle cardigan, and front teeth missing.

'Wasn't I an ugly brat?' Puts the brush on mantelpiece and slips coat on from behind door.

'We may just as well walk to his house.'

Hooks her arm into and 'Mam's not a bad old stick really, it's Paddy that I can't stand, although it's not his fault I suppose . . . he gets so cross at times.'

Then 'You know all about's a-cackle at me marrying a protestant, but I don't give a fig for them I love you.'

She turns to and puts her arms around kisses, 'I never thought I'd ever feel this way.'

'Some say you're fifty with a beard down to feet. Only after one thing, and will soon tire when get that, O their wicked tongues . . .'

And looking back suddenly is a face behind hedge — quickly dips out of sight. Grotesque. Face of all that's rotten in Ireland.

The housekeeper shows to a cold waiting room, looking closely at, plugs in a single bar of heat. 'Father's just having a bath, He'll be with you soon.' And leaves.

Eileen doesn't say a word but stares at her ring. There is a plate of breasts and palm branch facing, roses entwined on pale yellow wallpaper, Kilkenny Products calendar shows October and view of the Curragh. Tin of Quality Street by the coal bucket, cartons of tipped and plain cigarettes, box of Cuban cigars and that must have been his final year at Maynooth 1926. Nothing really personal or of interest would have gathered in travels surely, not even a book. Room comfortable enough . . . yet a place that is so empty . . . is it love that is missing?

The door opens and Father Keane — short, pinkish and grey, smelling sweet and well soaped enters offering hand, 'So you're the young man that wants to marry Eileen.' Looking at Eileen 'And how are you Eileen? Haven't been seeing you at Mass so much, now don't be neglecting us.'

'No Father.'

Beats a cushion, settles himself in chair, offers cigarettes and lights one for himself, inhales deeply . . . fixes eyes upon and picking words carefully 'Our Church doesn't normally encourage mixed marriages, but in this affair perhaps there's a case. I've known Eileen and her circumstances since a child and on the whole we would not be against her advancement. Of course any children of the union would be brought up as catholics and will need your real mother's written consent as you are still a minor Eileen.'

Looking most upset.

'Now you'll have to be nice to her this time, no priest could marry without it. The marriage would be in the vestry, purely symbolic of the Church's disapproval of such a union; think nothing of it. But, before we come to any of that I'll have to see the new bishop first about a dispensation, have an appointment with him next week, I will ask him then.'

The Church Munificent is carved on his forehead!

Waits for a moment as if letting words sink in, stands up and 'His Grace will probably insist that you take instructions of some kind if he does grant permission, but we can arrange that later on.'

Silence.

Even the voices are still, her heart has seen to that.

Spots Eileen's ring and bending to. 'My o my that's a very fine ring, your silversmith's work no doubt?'

Lifts her hand and inspects closely . . . and think she's so lovely and all things to, smiling again and surely God is in her at the feet of this cold man can only pity now.

'It's confession this evening, I must go, I'll be seeing you if it please God . . . goodnight.' Lets out, it is completely dark . . . and Mam is delighted.

'Sure didn't I tell ye Eileen when Father would meet him, would be a different story.' Makes tea with Marietta biscuits, she certainly doesn't care, character all right, a benevolent witch. Worked in the castle, used to starch Lord Ormonde's shirts, and remembers the last night of old century he gave a great firework display. Paddy nods asleep, Eileen looks bored, soaks cotton wool in a drop of whiskey and dabs on back tooth, shows where needs a good sized filling.

'They'll give ye no peace till they're all out.' Says Mam with experience and finality.

God no . . . might be just an idea to take her up to the North, could see own dentist does a good job, filling and complete check-up mightn't cost a penny on the National Health too! Have to meet parents sometime, only fair to let them know now.

Through Kilkenny in the headlights for a mad instant sway Hitchcock and Dunne. Wave to, call to stop.

Hitchcock leans his beery mouth in.

'We heard you're going to marry her, are you daft man, thought you're only having it regular, for Christ's sake I never.' Dunne shakes his head grinning silly, they'll be going up to their cold room for coffee now, will let them . . . until finally.

'Well anyway I'll expect an invitation to the wedding, Good luck whatever.' Says Hitchcock.

Dunne thumps the car roof and can see them in the rear view mirror crossing The Parade like two puppets on a string.

Couldn't be without her, not now. Will live in Mooney for a while, perhaps move to Kilkenny or even Dublin if she wants to . . . suppose it's only right should sign the paper and all . . . for her! Think nothing of it, in the vestry indeed!

They'd say the devil has a pretty face!

Monday — make a triangle of fifteen heads, melt silver into balls on charcoal and while still molten squeeze with parallel pliers at one end becomes skull like and bearded, texture, drill eyes and mouths with expressions of all mankind. Will stare out imponderable long after gone, small art, insignificant whim of one who passed this way; make and hang on a plain ring chain.

Tuesday, stands on a lonely shore, the sun is a citrine.

Wednesday a baby is baptized Shaun.

Thursday brings the clergyman. Smiling, obviously something on his mind though.

'Busy as ever I see, you seem to be doing very well . . . and before I forget, Mrs Haughton thought the box a very fine piece of work.' Brings out wallet and lays a pink Ulster Bank cheque on table. 'Told me to give you this.'

And then as if reluctantly, 'I hear you're getting married . . . to a Roman!'

And offering no comment.

'Are you really sure? It's a once in a lifetime step, and the children, think of the children, there's few enough of us left as it is.'

Still remaining silent, perhaps looking angry.

'I can see the matter's gone beyond reason, women are a very strong force.' Is he thinking of his own wife Margaret? 'I'll say no more, but do consider the matter most carefully, if we can do anything for you, don't hesitate to call.'

In the street turns, 'May God grant you happiness in all things.'

Hear car start and fade away . . . and the anger has gone, just a kind of sadness about Mooney today. Day that's bursting with the full glory of autumn, pigeons and magpies circle above, strong sunlight touches everything without shadows, cattle munch the pale blue hills, someone is cutting grass over grave. Maggie Anne clutching loaf and *The Kilkenny People* is in deep conversation with Brennan, probably saw him leave. What do they really think of it all?

Friday head for Dublin and the North, now Eileen's a little worried, but enjoying the change. At the Shelbourne Grill, again that cosy feeling, shrimp cocktail and a thick steak for her. Drogheda, Dundalk stop and buy Finn sticks of peggy's leg, always liked that. Through the gap of mountains, across Border and into County Down . . . think how neat everything is, been a while now, farms like well cared for gardens, an industrious made patchwork quilt. It is the first time that Eileen has seen the Union Jack flying.

Stopping for petrol in Castlewellan picks Mam a postcard of The Mournes and posts, asks why does the constable carry a gun?

At Ballylaneen father is clipping the drive hedges, comes into the yard. Mother from house, friendly enough to her but doesn't shake hands. Showing to room can just hear father say 'She's a pretty girl.' And mother 'Aren't they all.'

Sitting down to tea tell of plans to get married . . . father steals a kiss and 'I always wanted an Irish daughter-in-law.' Carves into pork pie, Eileen laughs nervously.

Mother looks at intently, with coat off now, 'Is that a pioneer pin you're wearing?

'Yes.' Almost defiantly.

O God . . .

After tea manages to get alone. 'I hope you're not going to do anything rash, she's still only a child, hardly knows her own mind yet. Mixed marriages, do you realize what that means?'

. . . shaking her head and certainly not accepting. 'Will talk about it more in the morning.'

Triumphantly finds a flea on her pillow, shows, as if to say what can you expect from a catholic! 'Was the same when took down to Dublin during the war, only two nights and head covered, had to buy a fine ivory comb.' Finds after all these years, hands to, 'She can have this.'

And that one little flea has justified all her feelings about the South, about catholics — an unclean inferior race — are the natives of Ireland.

Probably picked up from old Paddy or the goat, never did anyone a bit of harm. Is furious when give to, sobs when find another . . . but father makes her laugh at breakfast, is half the battle won.

Out of the dentist's together meet Finn coming in, looks much the same, head of prophet, stern preacher in baggy black flannel; smile fades as can clearly see spot her dark looks, from the Free State with that pin, and engagement ring on, hardly stops, just quick 'Hello there'. To her sin is the devil incarnate lured away to scarlet woman, lost forever . . . and probably on the National Health too, just typical, have they no pride?

And it hurts to realize have lost the first friend ever had. How would think it great and banged spoon when he raised his jug of buttermilk and in a loud voice that toast know so well.

> 'To the pious, glorious and immortal memory of William, Prince of Orange who came from Holland to save us from Popery, brass money and wooden shoes, and gave to us our freedom and an open Bible; and he will not drink this toast may be damned, rammed and crammed into the great gun of Athlone and shot from there into Hell, into the hottest part of Hell, with the door locked behind him and the key in an Orangeman's pocket.'

Will go on over to old home anyhow. Full of pigs all sizes, sows in the kitchen, dining and sitting rooms, weaners upstairs, one with an old pair of Auntie Annie's pink corsets shaking, ridiculous sight. Broken bed used to lie, wall where shadows of strange things crept while the boy slept. Everything brings a memory . . . and from that bedroom window can see the new Spanish style and green roofed house some fields away moved into last year. It is sore and ugly, his big metallic Zephyr drives up to, gets out, can see them all sit down to dinner. Good idea suppose not to waste the old house — fill with pigs, such a good price now . . .

Eileen's found an old book which she opens and over her shoulder read —

> The angry pontiff had them seized as they left the consistory and thrust into an abandoned cistern in the castle . . . The methods taught by the inquisitors were brought into play . . . Urban instructed the work to an ancient pirate, with instructions to apply the torture till he could hear the victim howl; the Pope paced the garden under the window of the torture-chamber, reading his breviary aloud that the sound of his voice might keep the executioner reminded of his instructions. The strappado and rack were applied by turns, but though the victim was old and sickly, nothing could be wrenched from him save the ejaculation, 'Christ suffered for us!'

> . . . made to stand upon a couple of faggots and tightly bound to a thick post with ropes . . . faggots mixed with straw were piled around him to the chin . . . clapped their hands, which was the signal for the executioners to light the pile. After it had burned away there followed the revolting process requisite to utterly destroy the half-burned body — separating it in pieces, breaking up the bones and throwing the fragments and viscera on a fresh fire of logs . . .

'The Lord save us!' and snaps it shut throwing away.

And as if a kind of symbolic sacrifice go down and fetch the peggy's leg. Unwrap the sticky brown sticks and lay on

110

cracked plate the three legged kitchen table. Finn will find them and know . . . the pigs and rats will eat them!

Haven't the heart to dander places hardly identify now. Pass the sprawling piggeries and henhouses, take her nowhere in particular, doze about . . . and coming near the old farm again stop, can hear music faintly. Creeping through the pine plantation together peer from behind trees . . . by far hedge is Finn marching up and down with bag-pipes wailing a glorious tune . . . there's no denying that music . . .

Eileen turns to eyes wide, 'Is he crackers?'

Wee William follows beating a drum!

Makes an extraordinary picture, picture seen many times before, but this time it is different . . . from generation to generation passed. Watch hypnotized until he stops, then slowly creep through covering and away.

Father likes without a doubt, finally tells mother to let be. And leaving he slips Eileen five pounds, wants to come back soon, mother is in her room! Take the coast road this time, show her more of the scenery, and driving one side of Ballyduggan Lake notice the boat in middle. It is Finn fishing, casts his silvery spoon and reels in. Park by little inlet where ducks gather for bread. The solitary figure on the dark lake that reflects a dull sky and tiny hills, sole commuter with his wrathful God. Sit on the front mudguard . . . and turning slightly spies for an instant, eyes meet, raise hand and wave . . . he does not acknowledge. Casts again and again . . . and sickness invades . . . for Finn who was all, had the ear of God, as Moses, best farmer, piper and shot in the whole county, is a fool!

And yet that man was King of all Ireland once!

And in front of him, all Ulster hold catholic Eileen Cumiskey and kiss, kiss, kiss . . . and her tears are your tears today!

On a tree someone has nailed — red on white
FLEE FROM THE WRATH TO COME

Back at the cottage Mam is beaming 'Father called, says it's

111

going to be all right, wants to see again on Tuesday, can call anytime.'

The new bishop was most benign, listened very carefully, and after considering Eileen's position would be most happy to see her progress! Usual conditions though, sign paper on any children, service in the vestry, mother's consent and catholic instructions from a Father Gleeson in Kilkenny.

Asks, 'Ever think of turning?' . . .

Muses 'No: You know it only comes with time. Perhaps one day you'll see our faith in a different light, always believe it makes more natural when the husband's same as wife. However we can't force you into that.' Smiling.

And think they're more than generous these days!

So dutifully every Thursday evening to Father Gleeson, seems a whole house of priests on the Ormonde Road. Opposite stubby tower and old city wall, is a pipe smoking young priest for his church, can't argue there; has faith to move mountains, his God is all things, seasons, song of blackbird . . . reads.

> 'Enter ye in at the strait gate: for wide is the gate, and broad is the way, that leadeth to destruction, and many there be which go in thereat: Because strait is the gate, and narrow is the way, which leadeth unto life; and few there be that find it.'

Mostly agreeing and trying to look interested, question here and there, he's certainly no listener, thoroughly enjoying himself seems . . . on and on and thoughts wander.

Pope Paul III had four children by a Roman gentlewoman.

Surely an historical figure?

Saw a brain in vinegar once!

Death is an eternity of unborn, the moon is made of pumice; commands a great conspiracy of silence, erosion and corrosion, everything disintegrates.

Tummy rumbles.

Widow's hump and a decayed tooth!

Could say his mouth is almost like a talking arsehole, ears too large, thick dandruff all around collar, beats pipe on back of shoe, scrapes with pen-knife and slowly fills from a tartan pouch. Strikes match and holding too long burns fingers a foretaste of hell. Another does the trick, sucks bowl to life, a glowing little ball in the near dark room now. Just whites of eyes and words, occasional car passes outside.

Will he ever stop?

Must surely realise there'll never be an answer, is it that important? . . . really a question of man needing myths to frighten off the devils of doubt and uncertainty — why are we here and where are we going? Pie in the sky if well behaved in this. If you can't give them bread, give them circuses and hope. Converse is sold by its main rivals communism and socialism which offer the deal here and almost now. The Church for small payments offers eternity, whose bargain looks best? None of us will ever know, so the old firm's claims can never be contraversed.

Prisoners, we're all prisoners of the dead . . . the autumn leaves swirl about everywhere, make a soft rustling and looking over the bridge at Inistioge the Nore is full after rain and from pocket take out paperbacks by Newman and Aquinas he gave . . . throw them down into, fine words and all to a watery grave!

Mam tells how to get there while Eileen reluctantly makes ready. Mother long married, lives down Waterford way.

'Don't have to worry about a thing now, there's good blood in her veins!' As comes down stairs, does she mean by that? Leaving . . . perhaps knows who her father is.

Knocktopher turn at the foggy road, rocky land, scrub and thorns grow, scrawny sheep graze about abandoned quarries. Looking grim . . . she's hardly said a word all day. To dull new council cottage with potatoes and cabbages growing untidy in the front. New crazy path leads to. Not in, children stare, Eileen's features, yet half is missing! Saturday and mother be at the chapel cleaning.

And Eileen's sitting in the car looking straight ahead, like a demon, would eat you alive!

On up the way rises to chapel, high nelly bicycle leans to ditch one side. Vestry empty, be married in such a storage space . . . woman on her knees near altar is polishing brass railings, turns startled looking up. 'You gave me an awful fright.'

Mother all right . . . but thicker, bigger boned, a country girl. Around forty say and seeing Eileen looking from door, gathers Brasso and cleaning rags into a wooden box and stands up, 'It's the first time you ever came to see me; and I think I know the reason why you're here today.'

Eileen turns away.

Sad and resigned then, asks back to cottage for talk and tea.

Sit each end of the table as she busies with plates and kettle on. Count five, six, seven or so children in and out shyly until she shoos away to play outside. Asks Eileen how been keeping, sends her regards to Mam and Paddy. Answers short, bit hard on her really. Pours tea with plate of sliced barm brack. The floors are concrete covered with bright linoleum, be a tight fit nearly ten a house this size. A yellow Kosangas bottle is attached to a half stove. Few pieces of O'Carroll's cheapest furniture, plastered walls not even painted yet, wonder where her husband is? Goes to another room and returns with a tin which she opens and shows some photographs of Eileen. God the little devil pretty as a peach then too. Must have felt all along for her to keep those, Eileen doesn't look at them, but makes a sign to hurry up. Would only have been about twenty time it all happened . . . and that remark of Mam's! But as Eileen would say, 'What's past is past, don't want to know.'

Is glad that Eileen is going to marry such a nice young man!

'Yes yes, there's nothing like a love match!'

Will sign on the dotted line . . . and the priest will be content, sealed in an envelope . . . her sin!

'Look after her now, she's a strong willed girl, but deserves

114

all the happiness can get.'

Comes out to car eyes wet, Eileen's face set. Waves . . . would she have approved if known was a protestant?

There's a hardness in Eileen, certainly knows her own mind, but she's smiling again now, planning her new home. Wants an old pine dresser with blue crockery on.

On a gable in Stonyford read —

TIME AND TIDE WAIT FOR NO MAN
and Tyres don't last forever
FIT Kilkenny REMOULDS

It will soon be Christmas, very cold and bright weather, clear frosty nights with Eileen these times when all is a kind of enchanted land, the precious meetings and mad dances the forgotten places. Driving her home under a cloudless sky the ground is hard white — colours the diamond on her finger, stars, moon and worlds away. Aware yet unaware . . . all will pass, her, happiness, Ireland!

The jewellery's selling quite well, she can start to buy a few things for the house. To seems like every shop in Dublin, she must compare and get what's just right. Following the proud old medalled IRA man about Kilmainham Jail, all hats off underneath the flag at half mast drooped wet against sooty grey walls in yard where men of sixteen were executed. And think of blood, Ireland and the catholic religion. Belong anywhere in this island? The world?

Gets a Christmas job in Woolworth's Kilkenny to be nearer. Gather holly in the grounds about the old brick shell of Woodstock House, Inistioge. And with streamers blue, red, yellow and few balloons tie all over house weekend before Christmas. Find in the Monster House for her a coat with fur collar and latest tall leather boots that zip sideways, all wrapped in bells and mistletoe. Small turkey, sprouts and potatoes, plum pudding, thick iced cake and midnight Mass the Black Abbey is packed, returns to Mooney with.

Will stay three nights, nice to have her about, a faint perfume and things put away, she's rearranging everything, looks much better.

Christmas day, trying hard to snow. Get a good fire going, busies with the dinner, calls in to taste thick brandy butter and sweetened cream. Looking out across the low rolling hills nothing moves, beside the faded pages lie.

I SING of a maiden
        That is makeles;
King of all kings
        To her son she ches.

He came al so still
        There his mother was,
As dew in April
        That falleth on the grass.

He came al so still
        To his mother's bour,
As dew in April
        That falleth on the flour

He came al so still
        There his mother lay,
As dew in April
        That falleth in the spray.

Mother and maiden
        Was never none but she;
Well may such a lady
        Goddes mother be.

Masses opposite . . . Finn could pick them off like pigeons! By three are the only ones in the whole world left. Just before meal give presents. Unwrap a striped shirt and thick gloves. Thrilled puts on boots and coat to see . . . is strangely out of

116

place, a fine bred lady now this wee house. One is dining with a princess, and as if knowing the effect leaves on and brings in the turkey soft brown and glistening. Flesh crumbles to sharp knife, she won't have any wine but lemonade instead. Set pudding on fire with brandy makes a blue flame, sliced with spoon of cream and good strong tea.

Not really caring who knows or sees now, with new gloves wearing walk out of village together, a magpie flies across.

'One for sorrow.' Says.

Looking at.

'One for sorrow, two for joy, three for a wedding and four for a boy, five for silver, six for gold and seven for a secret that will never be told.'

Noticed that about Eileen, superstitious . . . and walking back in the fast falling light cannot find another magpie!

When cutting the cake she carefully removes Father Christmas, reindeers, tree and puts them on the mantelpiece. Tastes so good with more tea after long walk. Stoke the fire up again and watch late . . . it is slipping so quickly . . . in the morning some of the streamers have fallen and turkey left in oven all night on low has shrunk to chicken size, with fingers eat for breakfast.

New Year's Eve finally snows, and first day of new year Kilkenny lies subdued under a thick covering. Pipes frozen, fetch water for Maggie Anne wrapped in two coats, can't see Eileen for a week, will get married in the spring soon, go away for short holiday together. Then the rain empties upon and turns all to slush, land a sponge that will take no more. The Father Christmas, tree and reindeers are still on the mantelpiece.

Fashion solemn men about unknown business, their horizon is endless and always night.

An army of protestants on the march — surly, self righteous, distraught . . . capable of anything!

She is twenty-eight miles away as the crow flies, could walk that rainbow to her. And the wedding ring make in plain wide polished silver.

Sight hurrying along caught in the shower to Freshford, soaked and alive, her words are like music. Last class of instructions over yesterday, leave another of his books on a stone beside Fertagh Round Tower. Picks the last day of April, just two witnesses, girl friend of hers and . . . Hitchcock would surely do. At Burke's she has made a suit of white Donegal tweed and dark blue wild silk blouse, shoes, hat and bag same colour. A week on the Aran Islands after. Father Keane makes a note in his diary and sign the silly paper . . .

'McCreery's are having a carpet sale, we could get a nice bit of green for the sitting room, let's go and see.' She says.

Slowly dress to wedding day — cloudless and dissolving lemony to chalk blue, each task is with deliberation. Coffee, two pieces of white bread spread with honey and banana. Another cup as polish shoes, shave, tie on, no not the old school crosses, something much more gay. Eileen be coming back so tidy up a bit, silver into loose floor board very neat, ring, money for priest, she said at least ten — too much, count three dirty English singles, better lick envelope shut, when he opens will be well gone, he's done well enough over the years. Bag of things right, curtains drawn, back and front doors locked, key with Maggie Anne, 'O such a great day to be getting married, will be looking forward to the new wife coming soon . . . good luck.'

Hitchcock on the hotel steps is waiting with a big covered basket lunch and two bottles of wine between feet. Obviously out to enjoy himself, spruced in loud cloth and beaming 'I'll follow in the van, it's too early yet, stop at the Rock Bar for a quick one.'

On the road to Freshford so many times before, could drive almost blindfolded, there's the spot where almost landed in the ditch asleep. Cool in the bar a large sweet sherry each take out to back, in the warm sunshine sit on empty crates, a suspicious hen clucks and keeps a button eye on. River Nore end of field sparkles wide from Bloom mountains, there isn't even a breeze . . . in the middle of Ireland to marry when the blackthorn is blooming. Even gotten to Dave draining his glass. 'There's no place like it on a fine day!'

Then 'As best man it's my duty to say you're not bound to marry the girl, could still change your mind yet. Are you absolutely certain?' . . .

Grins 'Come on now, we don't want to keep the lady waiting.'

Freshford's just beginning to stir, turn off at the Romanesque fronted protestant church, old man raises hand and puzzled gazes after. Mile or two and chapel up from the crossroads, no one is about.

Will she come?

Wait inside, up near front on right. Sunlight slants through the narrow windows like bars of gold, Christ on the way to Calvary stumbles and Veronica wipes his face. Rustling from vestry be Father preparing, give ring to Dave, seems in a trance at the altar crucifix.

Place where Eileen worshipped for the last twelve years from an unwanted child to this final insult at. There's someone on the balcony above . . . minding her own business!

Door at back opens and Eileen with her friend enters . . . just look at her, change your mind indeed. Her happiness radiating comes to beside and sits in pew opposite across aisle. Silence, glances like electric and Dave whispering 'You're a bloody lucky man.'

Father in robes appears left side of altar and beckons both parties to follow. Room is very small . . . are brooms, buckets and brass vases, fire extinguisher, boxes of candles, wine, oil, drawers open to vestments of white, green, violet and black; ledger on top of an old fashioned safe. Crowded begins in Latin from book. He has marmalade on his lip quite clearly — yellowish, sticky and sweet, has he washed? . . . as gabbles the dead words . . .

'I will.'

'I will.'

No change in pockets for to bless, Dave has half a crown,

be poor for life!

All sign the register in green ink, hand envelope to him . . . little crowd at gate has collected. Mam, Paddy Kennedy, don't know the others crowding in, wishing well, waving . . . the weather so perfect with Eileen beside as wife now, Dave and girl following.

She turns to 'I love you'. Then 'You know it wouldn't bother me if I never went to church again . . . ever!'

Stop by Durrow, sloping fields to river again. Plant wine bottles in soft bank under water to cool. Spread table-cloth starched white and stiff over grass where shamrocks are growing. On paper plates put cold chicken, potato salad, fresh rolls, golden butter, cucumber, barely ripe tomatoes and condiments. Only sounds river and birds in fuchsia, there are sows under willows in mud baths have made. Dave the proper gentleman spreads coat for Mary O'Brien to sit, doing very nicely for himself, fetch the wine bottles not much cooler, screw and pop corks, fill four glasses the red liquid; Eileen's first drink, wrinkles nose but perseveres.

## SALUTE THIS DAY

Picnic is a celebration feast this coming together, little conversation as perhaps each realising that today, uneventful, to most the same as before, unremembered yet all the more as will be forgotten. Lost in the sands of time. Who could ever find these precious minutes again?

. . . place seen nothing more dramatic than a couple of friars fighting, Abbot of Odorney on donkey bless a man covered with sores. Pour the last drop as it is time to leave, gather remains, shake cloth and pack all back in basket.

Dave will see Mary back with a wink, farewell on the bridge. Notice the sows are sitting up on haunches staring over, are the only ones that saw!

Up through the middle counties, over Shannon and by evening Galway, in the sanctuary of a small hotel room . . . to the

121

night clouding, a birth and death together warm and one the world is ending.

Hurry on board the *Naomh Eanna* to Arans, it has turned very cold, colder steaming into Galway Bay, flag ripping, high brownish green mountains rise up a wall from the sea in Clare. An expensively dressed American with long telescope scans the horizon . . . hands to his silk scarved blonde and tanned wife, their voices are an alien intrusion that reminds of reality . . . somewhere! Islands beginning are three pale hopes, propellers churn a long frothy path behind, go below and order tea, study passengers, unmistakable islanders, English, American, two young Germans equipped for anything study a map.

Whistle sounds, are nearing Inisheer, anchor is dropped as curraghs come out to meet, fragile as leaves look. From forward hold a reddish cow is lifted in sling and lowered into sea struggling fiercely, with rope around head is towed threshing towards island. Everyone is watching . . . at Inishmaan more curraghs and cargo unloaded, then into Killeany Bay and tying up at Kilronan pier under a mournful sky and shrill tumult of a thousand sea-gulls.

Quite a few people, piled lobster pots, ponies and traps, share the jaunting car with another couple, Eileen grips tightly, word with the driver in Irish, translates, 'Says it rained all day here yesterday!'

Clip clop along the pale sandy earth way to Kilmurvy, island's like a beggar's plate wiped clean, all bones and no flesh, not a single tree . . . was it right to bring her here? Gone somewhere livelier, more people, things to see and do . . . only nature's terrible monotony, hard rock, and salty water.

Past cemetery of rusted iron railings and leaning monuments, sheltered shallow curved beach to solid box house with ground rising behind to fort of Dun Aengus. Woman expecting shows upstairs to large room with double and single bed, odd old dark furniture. Eileen tired lies on bed, take off her shoes and cover with blankets rub forehead, smiles . . . asleep, raining outside, someone with collie herding ewes and lambs. Hope not catching the flu, yesterday was probably too much for her.

Go out all afternoon, then down to tea at round table with two shared jaunting car with and a priest — knows all about the island and pronounces names right. Dun Aengus the huge semi-circular fort standing on the edge of a three hundred foot cliff dropping sheer into sea. Dun Onaght, Temple MacDuagh, Templenaneeve, Dun Oghil and church of Four Beautiful Saints. Stone, Bronze and Iron Age, the Fir Bolg . . . a puffing hole to God only knows what awful depths, to be careful.

Eileen doesn't eat much, he says Grace.

It has stopped raining and a thick mist covers everything, will go for a short walk before bed. Well covered make for beach, soft and sandy underfoot to water's edge the waves rush in and pull back bubbling white . . . there is an awful despair and melancholy about this place. Tiny boat in the void, nothingness, battered and kicked without a hope to fritter and dance life away on this rotten driftwood!

Yet there's hope, hope in Eileen, million to one chance the paths, immense scribble of lives, lines crossed and held fast to this, huddled the weirdscape, she gazes into the unknown, barely visible sea that moans . . . everywhere. Whole Irish nation past and present from Skibbereen to Malin Head in her veins flows, they go in endless procession rude carved, dressed in deer skin with tinkling bells, blood-thirsty Celts, treacherous Kings, Queens, harp players, Patrick leading droves of saints, bishops, holymen singing and praying, ravenous soldiers eating the dead, starved people, Brian Boru is the size of ten men, Vikings with plunder, marching long nosed Normans burning and building, the skippy dog, cat, raven and mouse, he totters shouting drunken abuse . . . Cromwell, King Billy on and on, banners gold and green, drums, pipes, bugles, with his barrow of rotten potatoes, evicted tenants, mad laughing and dancing to a blind fiddler, risen dead of every generation, Carson and a loyalist crowd, stumbling ever forward Hagen Hogan Logan

O'Reilly Malone Brennan Brophy Cahill Callaghan Carroll Cleary Dooley Dowling Doyle Donovan Murphy . . . the infant that was buried in Mooney a week old!

And slowly, ghost like out of the sea and mist a curragh lands, pulled ashore by two men, turned upside down spilling fish, head and shoulders under is carried away — now like a giant beetle. Kneel and inspect their slippery dead catch. Eileen looking down, 'The way of all flesh!'

Should never have come, needn't stay the full week.

Morning monotone of Mass said on the landing outside, bursting to go, still sleeping . . . another dull day but warmer, can go up to the big fort after breakfast maybe . . . never seen her like this before, so tired since yesterday. Last ones down, other tables empty, jaunting car outside for some leaving, still off food, feeling well rested though, up to exploring a bit to dinner.

Probably needs a good tonic, all the excitement . . . change.

The sky is calm, colour of annealed silver, sea mirror reflecting. Over acres of limestone rocks, innumerable stone walls climb up and up, the island is spinning aged bronze, ribbed and slashed with grey violet. First defensive ring of fort and jagged uprights make a great bed of agony, touching the knit stone touch the man that laid, his long obliterated skull. Through second and innermost ramparts, nearing on all fours go down carefully creep, on bellies look over cliff edge. The water boils so far below, would fall like a bullet, burst as sack of blood, few screaming gulls, scuttling rockfish all would disturb the passing, red quickly dissolving, become oceans, eat the whole island, world away in time.

Eileen quickly draws back, 'It terrifies me a sight like that, makes dizzy . . . all that way to go.'

So in slightly and lie backs to west wall, salty kisses, smell in her clothes and hair. Little pink and yellow orchids are growing out of crevices about, brave flowers, pick some for her button-hole . . . and as if a miracle the clouds thinning roll away to let the sun flood through and all is changed. The island radiates brightness, warmth, new colours, shimmering greens, stones are white, sea deep blue to racing light. Knowing have only few minutes quickly scramble to highest point and view across to Connemara, speck of boat with sail, down island, sharp horizon of Atlantic . . . America!

Next life . . . nearly there, could almost grasp with her . . . Eileen.

Eileen.

All that matters . . .

Sky suddenly shuts tight again and all is as before, the moment is gone, she catches hand, 'Let's go back tomorrow.'

Said as if knows the sun will never shine again!

Down emergency entrance the ambulance screeched to stop. Rear doors opened and stretcher carried into the big modern hospital, wheeled along a short square tunnel to emergency ward and then operating theatre. Masked, booted surgeons in green and white bend over the unconscious patient.

Patrolman in main lobby gives routine information, finishes off report and enters hours in note book. Chatting to the nurse says 'He really hit that side with a vengeance!'

In the small room alone now, images again flickering in the darkness of his brain . . . ceiling, shaded bulb, rubber tubes, bottle, stainless steel, clip board with paper on a hook . . . another hospital, St Luke's Kilkenny, Chinese doctor — whatever brought him to Ireland? Expressionless behind desk with file explains about Eileen, blood corpuscles, an excess of white over red, after extensive tests, then hesitates and, 'It's leukaemia.'

Leukaemia.

Doesn't signify, cure anything these days . . . about only two weeks to live! Hand a tube of tranquillizers to take.

Will go with her . . . fetches water and empties two of the half green black pills.

Gulp.

Dead.

Eileen dead . . . only spent a few weeks with in Mooney after

Arans, to leave so soon, she can't, unreasonable, absurd . . .

My God!

No!

No!

Why? Not even twenty, life for what, what purpose . . . anything?

'She's in no pain, none at all, I lost my own wife when the Japanese took Hong Kong.'

Grasp his hand and cry, cry . . . until the pills seem to dull, blur thoughts, hardly keep awake, on couch . . . will stay with her all the while, she needn't know.

Very pale now, losing weight, rings too big, child again so fragile looking . . . eyes closed, oblivious to the fine summer's day, roses out, blackbird drawing a fat worm from freshly mown lawn . . . summer will not live to see! Ridiculously patched doll brought from cottage propped on locker beside. Planned to add another room to the house, teach to drive, help with jewellery . . . do so many things together. Feel her pulse . . . beats sixty-seven to minute is normal enough, how the little hands move relentlessly, take all before, can count last of her days on fingers now. Be just a memory, stored impulses, complete destruction, absolute, total, wife for a summer's month, be bones when leaves start to fall again.

The pain.

Wicked pain at that, to rot, fill with worms, be like that hideous bogman in the National Museum.

It was October to May in the County Kilkenny . . . loved as could never love again.

Perishing before, cruel God; she wouldn't have gone back, yet she believes. Never doubts for a moment in spite of that farce in the vestry.

> I am the resurrection and the life, saith the Lord: he that believeth in me, though he were dead, yet shall he live: and whosoever liveth and believeth in me shall never die.

Opens her eyes, dopey looking, hardly focusing . . . weakly recognises, 'Any word from the builder yet? Be nice to get it all finished by winter.'

Winter.

Gone again before can answer . . . be undertaker seeing instead, the pills, three this time will really send, whole bottle . . . together could go.

Nightmare drive out to see Mam, not suspecting, she should know. The road only last month to get married, happiest day ever lived. Three pound priest's house, alone in cottage, immediately suspects something.

'I thought last night was her last in, is she all right?'

Slowly tell . . . and her big old body heaves and sobs, face buried in towel, must be about for half an hour, then rambles on about Eileen as a child making tea.

'And with the good blood as well, Tollemond blood paternal side, old Arthur is the father, the mother worked in the big house as a maid. Was told that first time went to see Eileen at the home.'

Big house towards Waterford, woman at lunch the clergyman, long black boxes the estate agents office . . . the daughter of Lord Tollemond!

Is dying in Kilkenny and he doesn't know!

Paddy Kennedy stumbles up the lane roaring drunk, Mam beats him away with a hazel broom.

Pray until dawn in the chapel at Mooney.


DEAD

In the night just after four . . . last time . . . covered with sheet, draw back slightly . . . the terrible finality, kiss both cheeks. Collect things, clothes, handbag, talc, perfume, odds and ends, suitcase full, she had so little.

Leave her rings on.

All empty, deserted, people have no substance, shadowy

figures the sympathetic words . . . meaning has gone. Undertaker will see to everything, fetch to Mooney tomorrow for Mass and burial, only right there, home she chose . . . for a day!

Father Bollard will be ready at eleven, will see about the grave immediately.

Hearse arrives, with Hitchcock, Dunne and Brennan shoulder the coffin into chapel, lay on trestles to altar. Mam, Maggie Anne fingering rosary, others knew at school probably . . . pills do the trick, bad dream — awake soon, her mother late an awful scene. Glad when over, be alone. Kneel, sit, half follow their responses, Dave's face is tears . . . was only yesterday . . . he raises the gilt chalice and drinks, His presence: believe and she is in heaven. ' . . . Verily I say unto thee, This day shalt thou be with me in paradise.'

Eileen.

Priest leading, lift the coffin and follow to graveyard, it is softly raining, two gulls on the chapel gable look down. Piled earth is damp, deep enough, gently lower and Tommy with ropes into the earth. Voice goes on, first shovel hits the white pine wood, scatters, then Tommy takes and quickly fills . . . now covered, level, sealed . . . they gradually leave.

Dave sees to house, wants to come back to Kilkenny and stay a while. No; will call soon . . . see Tommy as times before pack soil and re-lay sods, gather shovels and door . . . all to say lies there only circles of flowers.

More pills.

In the candle light read.

> Sleep on, my Love, in thy cold bed
> Never to be disquieted!
> My last goodnight! Thou will not wake
> Till I thy fate shall overtake:
> Till age, or grief, or sickness must
> Marry my body to that dust
> It so much loves; and fill the room

129

My heart keeps empty in thy tomb.
Stay for me there; I will not fail
To meet thee in that hollow Vale.
And think not much of my delay;
I am already on the way,
And follow thee with all the speed
Desire can make, or sorrow breed.
Each minute is a short degree,
And every hour a step towards thee.
At night when I betake to rest,
Next morn I rise nearer my west
Of life, almost by eight hour's sail
Than when sleep breathed his drowsy gale.

Thus from the sun my bottom steers,
And my day's compass downwards bears:
Nor labour I to stem the tide,
Through which to thee I swiftly glide.
'Tis true, with shame and grief I yield,
Thou, like the van, first took'st the field,
And gotten has the victory
In thus adventuring to die
Before me, whose more years might crave
A just precedence in the grave.
But hark! my pulse like a soft drum
Beats my approach, tells thee I come;
And slow howe'er my marches be,
I shall at last sit down by thee.
The thought of this bids me go on,
And wait my dissolution
With hopes and comfort. Dear (forgive
The crime), I am content to live
Divided, but with half a heart,
Till we shall meet and never part.

And a fitful moon beams upon her grave, graveyard, standing stone in the far field . . . all Ireland.

Summer half gone.

Last pills, won't give any more, and each day as if the last now. Hardly work, just enough to keep going, from bench always across to place where she lies, the grass has grown high, should cut, put up a small memorial.

Pointless really. Mother wants to leave, forget ever happened; becoming morbid, whole life ahead yet to lead. Thinks will become a kind of crank these parts. One has to get on, be a waste of God given talent.

God!

'Thy will be done, As it is in heaven.' Be Finn's reasoning. 'Sometimes these things happen for the best!'

Yet father was a protestant . . . ironic that, could look up in Debrett's or Burke's the library in Kilkenny. Whole page and a half, be the sixth Irish Baron, created 1774. Ballyhale House, Co. Kilkenny. Clubs, Kildare Street and Carlton. Coat of arms — Quarterly gules and azure, a cross engrailed ermine. The four balled coronet, motto 'Had rather die than be dishonoured'. Eton, Irish Guards both wars, succeeded his father 1945. Born 1897, been nearly fifty when Eileen was born. Should have known better . . . war was ending, wife rather past it and quite rightly so there's a time and place for everything is the golden rule. Different class for a bit of fun, two kinds of women, wife demure and the bedworthy animal! Most days for few months, then she never showed up . . . was pregnant or not?

His daughter was born in Roscrea!

He saw again few times about the village and looked straight through, he was made of ice . . . yet how he used to . . .

Family way back to 1287 in Somerset, be French Norman name like that, to Ireland in the seventeenth century with Cromwell, wounded at Drogheda, mostly army . . . all over the world, lots in Church, bishops, one even an Archbishop

131

of Armagh and Primate of all Ireland. First Baron an M.P. in the old Irish Parliament and a Privy Councillor.

Would like to see just once, wasn't at church that day. So Sunday morning drive down to Ballyhale, wait opposite gates, arms carved on pediment above. Be no more than twenty minutes if coming. House quite large, well proportioned, fanning steps to Palladian style double door. Which room, what window behind the atom splitting moment her life began, voracious sperm met egg, God leaping galaxies to touch?

An open backed van carrying milk crates enters and drives round to the back.

Girl riding bicycle comes down the drive and out on to the road . . . another maid, mother once!

The trees sigh and shake, it is well trodden land this, recalls an invader's march . . . lord's right!

Must have owned quite a few acres to support an establishment that size. The van leaves, then comes that same black Wolseley. Looks left and right, the resemblance is striking. Why not follow to church? Go in when service just started, leave before end, needn't meet any of them then; get a better look at him.

Organ playing as walk in, hardly dressed for the occasion, boldly up and slightly behind them sit. He turns to and again, wife gives a watery smile doesn't know what to make. In pale green suit and polished brogues, Guards' tie gives a sensible touch of colour, hardly looks age, wiry, type live to be a hundred.

Eileen's father.

He reads the Lessons, loud confident and clear . . . strong impulse to cry out 'ADULTERER!'

Second, and Third stand up, he stops . . . her flesh and blood, creator. Staring at, you could hear a feather falling . . . astonished faces, little gasps as turn and walk out of their protestant church forever!

Ireland, sell the house. Must go, don't want to, come sooner or later, can't stay in Mooney always, remains so near. Things that bring back all over the house, a long dark hair only yesterday. Miles away, so far can't easily come back . . . to Canada. Start from scratch, do anything, big country, wide open spaces, empty valleys no voices of the past.

In the grassy ruins lengthening shadows bring out the strange beast and human heads, interlacing patterns just about there, crucified Christ, blind, almost abstract the withered arms and deeply pitted surface. Crows have it all to themselves, sheep caught in blackberry bush free. Plenty of ripe ones pick, enough to make jam if Eileen still alive. Over a year now since all started . . . that tiny fast moving glint of silvery so high in the sky, trails four fine threads of exhaust merge into one becomes a long pinkening cloud from sun setting. Five or six hours all it takes these days, leave in the morning be back again for tea . . . clean break, new beginning . . . ending.

Little pub somewhere, someone is playing *The Wearing of the Green* on an accordion. Drink the black liquid down, down and another . . . she's dancing there right beside, music goes on and on, louder, quicker in the blood and beer and tears . . . and Ireland.

What have you done?

The moment was born . . . with Finn spreading dung in the wee back field, two ducks rise and circle away to the Mournes. Silence and green green May fields in sunshine after rain, Newcastle train on time . . . devil in the quarry never far, not a chance, those first years, will hold till last breath.

Give the tinker woman her clothes and shoes, would understand; such a blessing! Parker the estate agent has an enquiry from an English potter . . . will buy.

Dublin airport watch yellow topped men fuel the emerald striped Boeing called Padraig. Light suited Americans, Irish returning with relatives sad, girl right out of *Vogue* tapping her Pall Mall so expertly... call, last call for the flight about to leave.

The forced smile that welcomes, seat by window tail end, whine that grows as slowly turn, taxi, stop. Noise becomes a roar, whole plane shudders as if in final prayer, brakes off and away . . . free, airborne, a frightening angle of climb, whole country spreads rapidly; sea, lakes, mountains, so many shades into clouds . . . And soon only a thin finger of Ireland stretches into the grey Atlantic. From pouch in front take out the various brochures.

> No spot on Earth has had its praises sung and recorded in prose and poetry as has Ireland. Its glittering and brilliant colour, enchantment and magic, charm and hospitality are all true and reach out to visitors . . . to seekers of adventure behind a Shamrock Curtain. Your adventure may be a simple walk through the delightful countryside, or visits to the famous castles, homes and historic spots; fishing or swimming in the many beautiful lakes and streams; golfing; shopping or visiting the many pubs and fine restaurants. Whatever your pleasure, you're never far from the welcome of one . . .

What is one doing? Above the world, ocean of tears, so far

now from Ireland, will never return . . . someday perhaps, too late; the ever yearning, looking back — will eat a whole life away.

Can just make out snow covering and countless icy lakes, endless horizons of pine forests empty and void . . . dreaming her kisses again and again . . . and the engines' noise changes, fearfully the new world is coming relentless like the reaper. Would only be like this for all time suspended, become clouds and shifting air, arctic cold and sunlight raining with her. Can see houses and bright moving cars, another lake that's a sea and the earth races to hard amber slashed with the melting snow.

Could take the next plane back; no no must go. Hostess looking at, get up and out slowly down the metal steps an awful coldness hits, this world is forged and harsh and made of polished steel.

The immigration officer stamps passport IMMIGRANT — 'LANDED' IMMIGRANT — 'RECU'. Hands back to impassively and 'Good luck then.'

Where does one go?

Take that big silver bus somewhere; the highway is straight, six laned and so fast, shapes like angry sharks, could only drive on forever to: in downtown Toronto alone.

That hotel doesn't look too expensive, will do, anything will in a tiny room so high and the traffic faintly below; trapped in this cell, try to sleep . . . and a faint tapping, yes must be someone at the door.

Is a heavily made up blond, 'Can I come in?'

She sits on the bed and lights a cigarette quickly fills the air and her thick musky perfume. It will be fifteen dollars or fifty for the whole night . . . She's pretty in her hard kind of way, leaning on arm inhaling deeply, slowly folds the three five dollar notes into handbag.

The room is far too warm. Asks 'Where are you from?' And 'Why did you leave?'

135

It is all in slow motion . . .

Stubs cigarette out, stands up, takes off coat and drapes over the chair. Then white blouse and black skirt to flimsy red bra, panties and matching suspender belt. Her pubic hair is the colour of chestnuts, heart pounding this new dawn or night. Tears off clothes and she lying completely back, open those legs wide an altar go down and wet lips sweet and sour and protesting didn't pay for this, in vain, each breast and nipple now she's even wanting, can wait . . . her moans and own as into this mad relief's a dance of death leaping miles away . . . in her arms, the sweat is pouring.

Is anything real anymore?

Still undressed she lights another cigarette, and looking at 'You really needed that, didn't you?'

And looking over the room, 'Is that sink the only place there is to wash?'

Over it stands on one leg and soaps underneath. She looks so vulnerable now, the pale flesh is grotesque, sad mis-shapen form quickly dresses applies more make up and brushes hair into place. Snapping bag shut, 'See you then.' And she's away.

Did it really happen?

Go down and walk the streets of slush in any direction the rush of traffic and passing people. Order coffee and hamburger in a restaurant of seems only sad Greeks or are they Italians? Babble away incomprehensible. There's a juke box playing far too loud, old Chinaman outside, will have to get a job; could hardly make own silver for haven't the place or money to start.

Soldering parts together by the gross to be silver plated at eighty dollars a week. Working an elevator, selling shoes or reading meters, no. No money left at all go on like this asking policeman the way — does anyone know?

From Ballymena, wouldn't you guess and an ex RUC. Now there's an idea for a while perhaps, would be a start and lots of free time; could search the whole continent.

At the police college is easy enough. Few from the old sod, juvenile lot, East Coasters and clowns; learning to shoot straight, criminal code and powers of arrest.

Hardly hear the grizzled sergeant's words gazing out the window at spring in the woods, chipmunks runabout, all the snow has gone, warm and dry and an ever blue sky. Will drive far north the weekend. Hire a big Chevy Impala with radio, eight V cylinders, power brakes, steering and white wall tyres that squeal at the lightest touch.

So vast and seems almost untouched some hundred miles from the city in a canoe on a lake paddling towards a deserted island. Not a sound but birds, no sign of man, nothing's gone before, a few Indians and bears and an emptiness that's distressing. Throwing stones in the deep water and watching the ripples ring out and lap the sandy soil shore. With the end of a maple branch write her name . . . that the wind and rain and snow will take away by winter. View that wouldn't have changed since times of the great ice. Christ born in Bethlehem more snow and a dying moose.

Sleep in the car. Watching the slow woody smoke rise from campfires about, few voices and stars appearing, moon over the trees; does one really live? All's illusion, listening to that stupid music and message that never stops from so many different stations . . .

It is morning already, drive on to Drive In — so clean and such helpings, and well will maybe get used to eventually. Life is a challenge, fierce monotonous beauty of certainty. From that square tower with ivy growing two sides on a carpet of darkening greengold to river and sky varied greys breaking blue . . . Crossing more water in a ferry, soon be back this speed would hardly think was doing over ninety miles an hour!

And an apartment in a tower — there's constant hot water, heating, box for mail; swimming pool and laundromat ground floor, garbage very handy down a chute outside. The long corridors and numbered doors; people on all sides but completely unaware, could be dead for weeks. Watching television and drinking canned beer with savories dipped in soft cheese; in the big Power's supermarket whatever ones needs.

There's a nurse called Angelique from Quebec two floors above will let do anything with; to forget! Makes wonderful pizza and works the same odd hours.

As most junior walking Bloor Street from midnight to morning in a blue uniform the time can go so slow. Dozing in a hallway or garage talking to an imbecile watchman munching salami sandwiches the conversation is meaningless in the weird light. His false teeth are so white and fit badly, glasses reflecting are like two lemons.

'You're from the old country aren't you? Well my old pappy was from Bristol, came out as a lad the early part of this century, had a real tough time in those days, the trouble is now kids expect it all on a plate, those bearded wonders . . . in the thirties shovelling snow for . . .'

He's still talking to himself moving on, and only two o'clock. Time people die . . . sitting on crates back of a lane taking out .38 and flicking out the chamber. The six drilled holes and cartridges that fit so snug pulling back the firing pin to the head would be all over . . . is that scalped Patrol Sergeant looking for.

'Hop in I'll get you some coffee.'

Signing note book. He accelerates off to the back of Mario's all night, and think don't fat policemen look obscene! Disquieting shape with truncheon in back pocket and belly spilling over belt, he returns with two paper cups of coffee and when offer to pay looks at as if mad.

'Mario wouldn't charge a Po Lice for coffee.'

What does one talk about? Two souls in a mustard coloured Plymouth this hour sipping coffee and both are turned to stone!

He finally belches, crumples finished cup in hairy hand and

throws on back seat, fumbles for cigarettes in top pocket, offers and lights.

'And that's the way the cookie crumbles man, let's go!'

Back to the station for break, is like a house of the damned. Fluorescent blues and greeny greys; some at tables — heaped Sam Brown's and holsters, munching Chinese or Kentucky fried. Drunken yells from cells a rattling metal door and piercing 'Youse God damn mother fuckers, let me outa here!'

Laughter and duty sergeant's voice, 'Shut up Coaster!'

Willie Douglas fitfully sleeps slumped a guardroom chair. Wanted men are watching, giant of a sergeant strides in and pins new time sheet on cork board; blows a paper bag and bursts in Willie's ear.

'Come on Douglas, get after them ya God damn lazy Irishman!'

Visibly jumps, buttons top of pants that don't fit, loads revolver, jacket and cap on backwards grinning madly to the sergeant. 'I squeezed the nigger's balls till he was sick, be the last time he'll say I'm not with it, or call me a pig!'

Watch him in the square below filling Ford with gas; radio crackles a lost message and he's away.

At counter take any teletype messages, passing cells a figure at bars gripping shouts more drunken obscenities, skinny West Indian youth sobbing. In the D's office a Coaster is being beaten.

Out into the night again it is very cold, the first faint hope of dawn breaking. Should have stopped and summonsed there making No Left Turn, haven't the courage, will have to get a few by end of month. Scout car passes and loud Belfast voice shouts across, 'Ye'll freeze to death there boy, and only another five hours to go, he heee ee!'

Doesn't he play pipes in police band?

A distraught woman suddenly rushes to, 'He's dead, dead, the old man's dead, come quickly!'

Leads to side street and up wooden stairs. Some kind of

boarding house, few watching, one looks like an Indian at door. 'Didn't hear or see for few weeks, hadn't paid the rent so went in to see — my God! I'll be downstairs, but get him out of there right away!'

Room dark, can't see a thing, that smell . . . of death! No way out of it, light on. O Jesus God! Lies propped up on bed, head swollen a ghastly blueblack contrasts the growth of white stubble beard, eyes wide open staring . . . at picture on the facing wall. Picture of The Twelve Bens Connemara. The misty mountains ride on streaks of copper gold and mirror water, a thatched cottage catches the evening sun . . .

Body disintegrate try to move; write it all down as taught, phone for Patrol Sergeant and ambulance will take to morgue.

She says his name was Patrick Egan with no known next of kin.

Good to be out of that. Walking underneath the bridge there goes a slow rolling line of freight CN CN CN CN CN CN CN . . . whistle fills a thrilling note, of the West and ceaseless wanderer. The last star is just visible above the old ornate carved Imperial Bank of British North America.

It will probably snow, one's tears would freeze. Scrounging a coffee — warm cup brings life back to hands and Willie lifts back to station. 'Isn't it a dog's life weather like this?'

And he's right. Will have to leave, a pilgrimage to where?

Niagara Falls on day off, the water thunders and makes a rainbow, stars and stripes on the other side . . . with another and another drive anywhere is nowhere that loops on and on curving to big sweeping S over and under to another day like the one before.

In a foot of snow, the silent falling flakes blanket the whole sleeping city. In a patrol car at last slowly around the miles of railroad tracks, enormous silos of grain. Checking for no break-ins the Cloverdale Mall — shopping centre's deserted parking lot covers at least thirty acres, like grounds for some strange sport the receding white lines and arrows.

What civilization is this?

The things one sees. Like Pole who drowned in a vat of purple dye the other day was a life of singular purpose. Electrocuted to a cinder. Impaled on steering wheel. With everything she could possibly want, her life away on an overdose of sleeping pills. Hand caught in a lathe. Beserk whore clouted by PW with an iron hand. Dead dressed in diver's suit on a huge double bed.

'Scout car 224 call.' Cracks into thoughts with her about the Slieveardagh Hills when she . . .

'Go to 193 Kitchener Road re a parking complaint.'

And headlights bore into the darkness, rubber burns as swing into highway past Kentucky Fried Chicken, Gulf gas, Midas Muffler the neon colours shout the new message, a giant hot dog is sailing to the heavens, milk shakes and tyres, honest Coke . . . to a car that's where it shouldn't be. Write out the long yellow parking ticket. Voice from above shouts, 'Just how does that bum expect me to get outa there in the morning?'

There is an address somewhere, if can only find. That American who called in Mooney; Missouri wasn't it? M, M, Mev Meveral . . . yes, yes still in wallet gave that afternoon soon after arrived, bought the angel cuff-links. Very fancy —

MEVERAL B DREYFUS, INC
Diamonds and Rare Gems
909 NORTH TWELFTH STREET
SAINT LOUIS 1, MISSOURI

Said to write if ever thought of coming over. Thought work was so very different, will do that now. His suit was lightweight plum, edges double stitched and his grandmother came from Enniscorthy.

Is delighted and wants to come on down as soon as visa is granted.

He's waiting at Saint Louis airport, 'Hi there, so glad you came.' It is very hot as he leads to the two toned Cadillac with tinted glass . . . air conditioned, sweep through suburbs, black men drink beer from cans in gaudy pants and string vest tops, gaze from windows, half listening '. . . more I think about it, I'm just convinced you could fit into our organization fine . . . something positive to offer . . . new and different approach . . . able to sell . . . can contribute . . . and increase sales by at least . . .'

THE GREATER TRUE VINE SPIRITUAL CHURCH
Honour Duty Country
Go Army
Was Martha Washington George's wife?
Rifles, Shotguns, What Have You To Sell?
ONE NATION UNDER GOD
Caster-Fink Loans and Military Goods

Screw up and up the concrete parking tower, can just see the mud coloured Mississippi. The building's of sheer glass and vertical steel soars, gleams a kind of energy, the sun pierces everything, the new world is booming.

Elevator doesn't make a sound, few passengers mute, light stops at fifteen.

There is a diamond room, ruby, sapphire, emerald and gold. Carpet's thick as sheep's back, slim drawers reveal a king's ransom. A platinum blond is looking at diamond rings, some the size of her thumb nail, one enormous canary, the salesman's a sycophant shadow.

Can start right away, pay more than generous. Their interest in Ireland is almost bordering on the childish . . . at the Park Plaza . . . a solitary figure stops to light up under the blinking Avis sign. A black preacher at intersection below stands, eyes fire, teeth shining, voice sings out the message to gathered few 'Let not your heart be troubled: ye believe in God, believe also in me. In my Father's house

142

are many mansions: if it were not so, I would have told you. I go to prepare a place for you. And where I am, there ye may be also . . .'

From a photograph of Mrs Werner III's favourite horse design a near likeness in gold, diamonds and tiny ruby eyes, makes a three thousand dollar pin. Diamond and emerald tiger jewels. Ruby, diamond and cultured pearl buckle; diamond and sapphire duckling pin; diamond and cabochon emerald lion clip — NEWLY CAPTURED IN GOLD AND ENAMEL AND NOW IN OUR JEWELLED MENAGERIE.

Down at the riverfront, old steamboat turned into a restaurant in the umbrella shaded open eat. A plane is writing in the sky SEVEN UP! Big double locomotive parallel to river hauls more freight —

Pacific Fruit Express
Santa Fe — all the way
Armour
Southern Pacific
Southern Serves the South
Norfolk and Western
New York Central System
Delaware + Hudson
Pittsburg + Lake Erie
Beo
Penn Central
Rio Grande
Missouri Pacific Lines
Cotton Belt

She is just back from a holiday in Greece, and has come up to St Louis from Little Rock to buy a necklace; wife of a wealthy shoe manufacturer. Can see her hand the doorman of Mercantile Bank a dollar bill which will take care of Eldorado. Must be well over forty but certainly doesn't look it; smells a fortune, fastening catch, half down bosom revealed. Nothing in stock really to liking, will rustle some designs could make up, perhaps bring around tomorrow evening.

Some suite, kind of Wedgwood Georgian. Likes the one of interlocking figures, smiling, be a combination of pavé set diamonds and rich gold, excuses for a moment . . . and reappears nearly naked!

Way home detour to Forest Park . . . and remember remember, always remember!

Ireland!

Eileen!

Is there no future?

For the first generations?

The times least expecting creep the memories where all things began, will utterly destroy, eat away each year doing better and better with money to burn . . . The car beside two smart ladies from late closing Art Gallery clutching catalogues unlock.

'You're solid.'

'Yes I am, on Weight Watchers . . .'

Other side a man and his wife.

'My God, what do they want?'

'They're on aid. They don't work . . .'

For Mrs Schlapp an exquisite oval opal set with three small diamonds each side all on delicate white gold wires. Onyx poodle with golden thread tail, enamelled basket of flowers and dancing harlequin. Certainly has the customers to pay such prices.

For Christmas the Governor of Arkansas buys his wife the bracelet of all kinds of faces for fifty thousand dollars.

The months that turn to years, prosperous, uneventful, trip here and there . . . the live green pig led around Arland's on an orange sash by a miniskirted girl on Paddy's Day. Sounds of the Londonderry Air fill the whole supermarket, gleaming car park and try hard to hide back the tears tearing . . . there's Inistioge, across to Ballyhack recognise. A group in Aran sweaters, dark haired girl in red sings rather poorly, yet . . .

> 'I would I were on yonder hill,
> 'Tis there I'd sit and cry my fill,
> And every tear would turn a mill . . .'

And immediately order the new Pontiac Parisienne — fire red upholstered in white. Propose to his daughter, and house hunt in Creve Coeur.

On television they're burning Belfast down most evenings. A letter that father was shot through the throat by masked men looking for guns, mother's in the mental home cursing Fenians forever . . .

With the twenty-five carat pink diamond leave for Kansas City very early. Will more than likely buy.

Temperature's over ninety already, the land is an oven. Slight curve, he's too far over on the left overtaking fool, brake hard hard, too fast never make it . . . as good a way to go as any . . . America's heartland . . . so far away, no pain, none at all now . . . the soft darkness spreading, slipping fast, at last, long last for this hour to come . . .

The doctor said his injuries were not that great, was as if he didn't really want to live!

They dressed him in a good suit, powdered face and folded hands at rest the rich velvet lined coffin at the flowered funeral parlour with soft taped organ music; along with six others some days after. There came four car loads from St Louis, the girl wept on her father's arm. And that afternoon the gas flames leapt and ate the wood and flesh and bone so efficiently. Anything left was ground to finest dust and put in a marble vase in a recess the walls covered with creeper in the big garden of remembrance Kansas City . . . the moon rose early and turned the seas of wheat to silver.

Finn stood on top of Love's Hill and watched the sun rise on Ireland, thought it would be another fine day, day to start his own corn cutting.

> May the angels take you into paradise; may the martyrs come to welcome you on your way, and lead you into the holy city, Jerusalem. May the choir of angels welcome you, and with Lazarus who once was poor may you have everlasting rest.

*Acknowledgements*

Thanks are due for permission to use some of the quotations in this book: page 30, from *Celtic Mythology* by Proinsias MacCana, published by Hamlyn; page 37, from *Thessaurus* by Stokes and Strachan, published by Cambridge University Press; pages 61, 115 and 128 from *The Way to Poetry*, published by the English Universities Press (Hodder Educational). Every effort has been made to trace the owners of copyright material quoted in this book, and in the event of any omission having unintentionally been made, the publishers will be pleased to include an acknowledgement in any subsequent edition.

The publishers acknowledge the financial assistance of the Arts Council of Northern Ireland in the publication of this book.